GRAPHIC MODERN HISTORY: WORLD WAR II

THE SECRET WAR

By Gary Jeffrey & Illustrated by Emanuele Boccanfuso

 Crabtree Publishing Company
www.crabtreebooks.com

Crabtree Publishing Company

www.crabtreebooks.com

Created and produced by:

David West Children's Books

Project development, design, and concept:

David West Children's Books

Author and designer: Gary Jeffrey

Illustrator: Emanuele Boccanfuso

Editor: Lynn Peppas

Proofreader: Wendy Scavuzzo

Project coordinator: Kathy Middleton

Production and print coordinator:

Katherine Berti

Prepress technician: Katherine Berti

Photographs:

Bundesarchiv: pages 4t, p6t, p45, p45t

brewbooks: page 4m U.S. Air Force:

pages 5m, 45m U.S. Air Navy: 5b TSRL:

page 7br, Ed Westcott / US Army /

Manhattan Engineering District: page

44m U.S. Navy National Museum of

Naval Aviation: page 46 US Office of

Strategic Services page 47

Library and Archives Canada Cataloguing in Publication

CIP available at Library and Archives Canada

Library of Congress Cataloging-in-Publication Data

Jeffrey, Gary.
The secret war / Gary Jeffrey ; illustrated by Emanuele
Boccanfuso.
p. cm. -- (Graphic modern history. World war II)
Includes index.
ISBN 978-0-7787-4195-4 (reinforced library binding : alk.
paper) -- ISBN 978-0-7787-4202-9 (pbk. : alk. paper) -- ISBN
978-1-4271-7875-6 (electronic pdf) -- ISBN 978-1-4271-7990-6
(electronic html)
1. World War, 1939-1945--Secret service--Comic books, strips,
etc. 2. World War, 1939-1945--Secret service--Juvenile literature.
3. Graphic novels. I. Boccanfuso, Emanuele. II. Title.

D810.S7J39 2012
940.54'85--dc23

2011050089

Crabtree Publishing Company

www.crabtreebooks.com   1-800-387-7650

Printed in Canada/012012/MA20111130

Published in Canada
Crabtree Publishing
616 Welland Ave.
St. Catharines, Ontario
L2M 5V6

Published in the United States
Crabtree Publishing
PMB 59051
350 Fifth Avenue, 59th Floor
New York, New York 10118

Published in the United Kingdom
Crabtree Publishing
Maritime House
Basin Road North, Hove
BN41 1WR

Published in Australia
Crabtree Publishing
3 Charles Street
Coburg North
VIC 3058

CONTENTS

SIGNALS

On July 25, 1939, at Kabaty Woods near Pyry, in Poland, Polish cryptographers handed to the British and French equipment they had used to break Germany's Enigma code. Six days later, Poland was invaded and war was declared against Germany. The precious gift had not come a moment too soon.

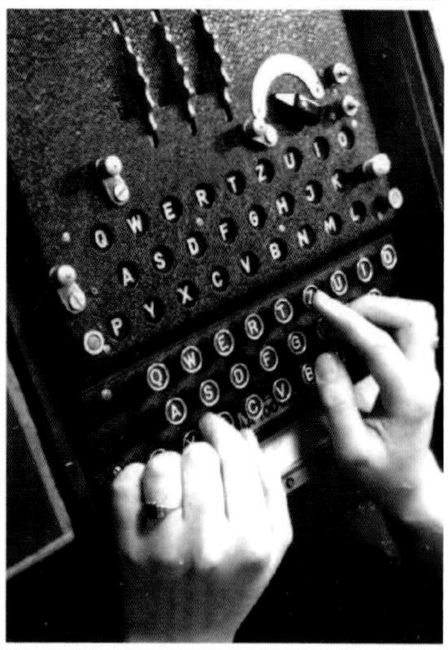

The German Enigma machine used rotors electrically connected to typewriter keys to encrypt messages in thousands of possible combinations.

Ultra Intelligence

The Poles had been studying the code traffic of their aggressive western neighbor for 10 years. They had constructed machines called bombes that would tirelessly work through all the possible rotor combinations. Their breakthroughs laid the foundation for wartime code breaking at the Government Code and Cypher School at Bletchley Park in Britain.

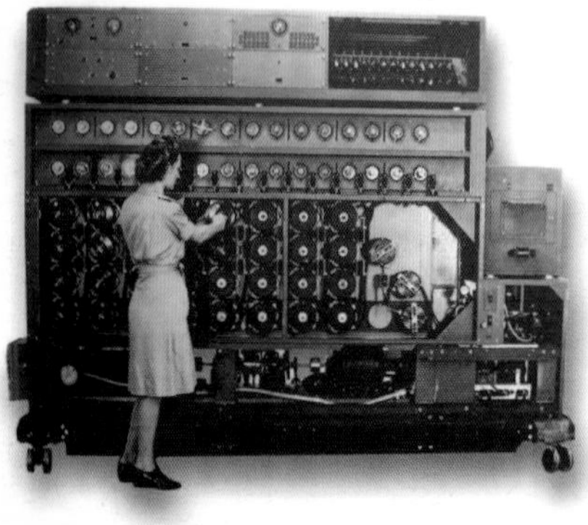

A US-made bombe for decrypting U-boat traffic

The intelligence that came out of Bletchley Park, code named "Ultra," was pioneered by civilians—some of whom were the most brilliant mathematicians in Britain. At its height, Station X, as it was known, was listening to and decoding 4,000 messages a day.

The detailed information on the movements and strength of German air force, army, and navy units proved invaluable. The achievement of keeping it secret from the Germans—priceless.

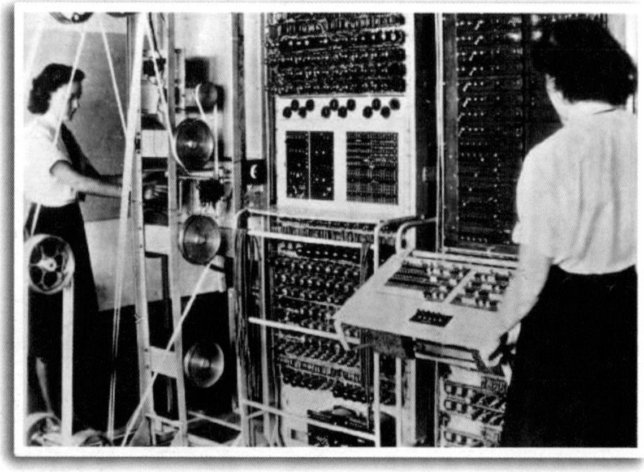

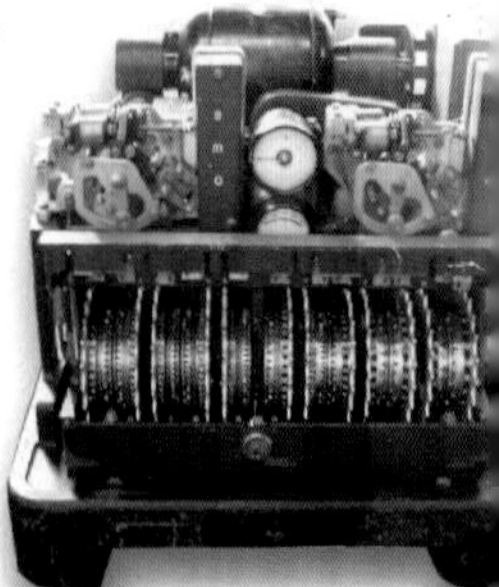

Near the end of the war, Colossus supercomputers (left) were used to decipher messages sent on Lorenz machines (right). In operation, the Lorenz would be connected to a teleprinter to communicate directly with German High Command.

Operation Vengeance

The United States had managed to break the main Japanese code (which was based on code books) in May 1942, enabling them to win a decisive victory against superior forces at the Battle of Midway (June 4–7, 1942). On April 14, 1943, they intercepted traffic regarding the travel arrangements of the Supreme Commander of the Japanese Navy, Admiral Isoroku Yamamoto.

President Franklin D. Roosevelt saw an opportunity to *"get Yamamoto"*—the man he felt was directly responsible for Pearl Harbor. Sixteen specially equipped P-38 Lightnings were ordered to take off from Guadalcanal for the longest fighter-intercept mission of World War II.

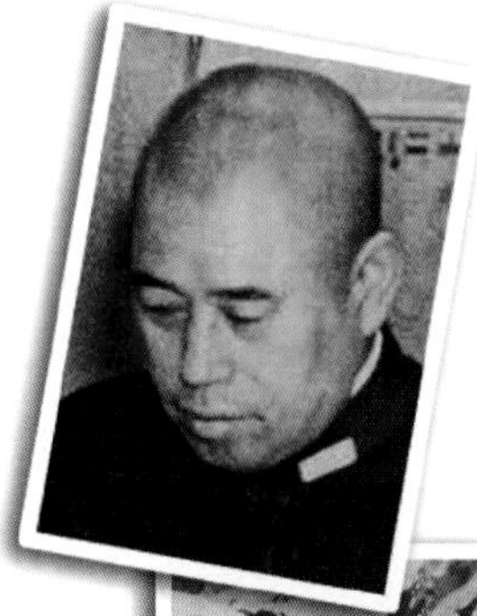

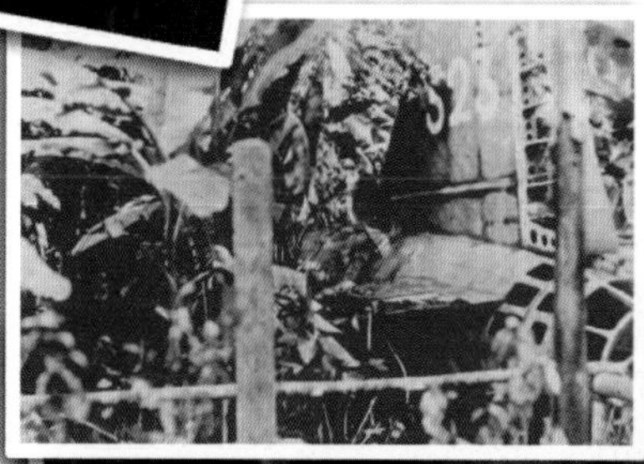

As Yamamoto's transport came into view over Bougainville Island on April 18, four P-38s—the "kill team"—dropped fuel tanks and climbed full throttle to intercept. Bullets riddled the fuselage and starboard engine of the Admiral's Mitsubishi G4M1, sending it crashing into the jungle (left), and killing Yamamoto instantly.

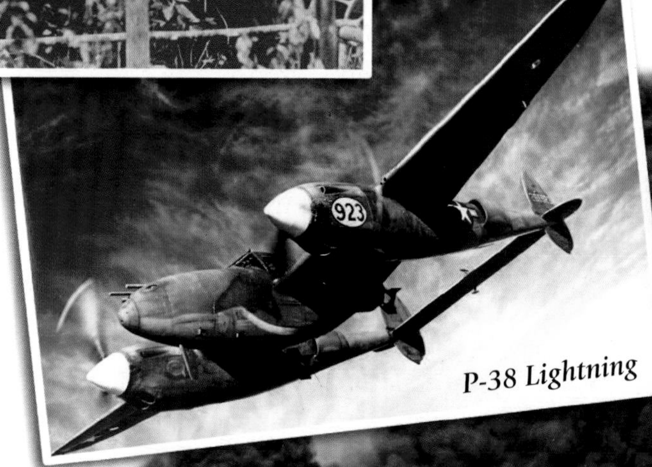
923

P-38 Lightning

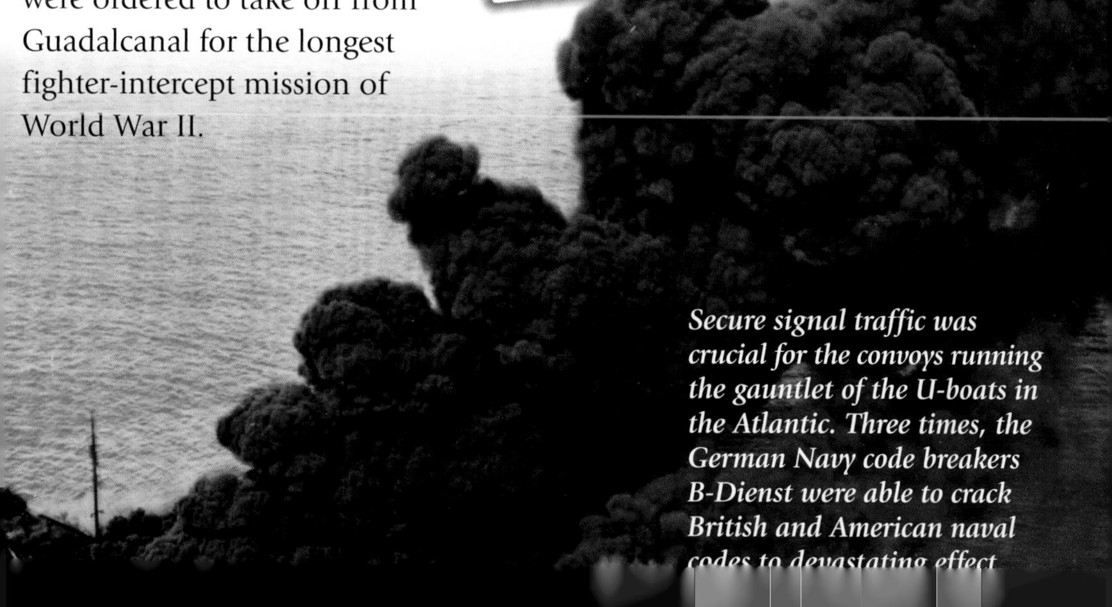

Secure signal traffic was crucial for the convoys running the gauntlet of the U-boats in the Atlantic. Three times, the German Navy code breakers B-Dienst were able to crack British and American naval codes to devastating effect.

SPIES AND SABOTEUR.

German-born Sorge had been spying for the Soviets since 1925, and was a master of the game.

In December 1940, Joseph Stalin got word that Germany was planning to attack the Soviet Union in the summer of 1941. It seemed unbelievable—Hitler had signed a non-aggression pact only the year before. The intelligence had come from a top Soviet agent in Japan, but Stalin ignored it. After all—how could he trust a spy?

MASTER SPY

The spy in question was Richard Sorge, a German journalist and member of the Nazi Party, who had spent seven years building up a network of operatives in Tokyo. As German forces steamrollered their way toward Moscow in August 1941, Sorge sent word that the Japanese did *not* intend to open a second front by attacking the Soviets through Asia, as was thought. Red Army troops were shifted west to help save Moscow, altering the course of the war.

Two months later, Sorge was arrested by the Japanese and offered in exchange for captured Japanese spies. The Soviet response was *"Who is Richard Sorge?"* The spy who had probably single-handedly changed history was executed in Japan on November 7, 1944.

DOUBLE-CROSS

Beginning in 1940, Germany's military secret service, the Abwehr, parachuted more than 100 agents into Britain. They were to report on home defenses for a possible German invasion, and eventually attempt sabotage. Not only were they all caught, but many were *turned*. In exchange for their lives, they were to help the security service, MI5, feed false information back to the Germans.

A handful were so good they became superspies. Agents "Tricycle," "Garbo," "Tate," and "Zigzag," spent 1942–43 convincing the Abwehr of their networks of imaginary agents. "Ultra" confirmed the bait was taken and, in 1944, this double-cross system played a large part in misleading the Germans about the planned landing site of D-Day.

Agent "Zigzag," the British criminal Eddie Chapman, even offered to try to kill Hitler in a suicide attack, if MI5 could get him close enough.

When six Abwehr agents arrived by U-boat to spy in the United States in 1942, their leader, George Dasch, gave himself up to the FBI. US attempts to infiltrate Nazi Europe worked better.

SPECIAL OPERATIONS

It was July 1940. France had fallen and the German air force was about to begin trying to pound Britain into surrender. Churchill wanted to fight back by waging a guerrilla war in France. The existing British Secret Intelligence Service (SIS) looked with alarm at the building of this "secret army"—the Special Operations Executive, but Churchill was determined to *"...set Europe ablaze!"*

Training bases were set up. Recruits came from all walks of life and all nationalities. Commando training, including unarmed combat and use of concealed weapons, was given. The German secret police—the Gestapo—along with the Nazi army—the SS—would show no mercy to any operatives they captured.

New Zealander Nancy Wake was nicknamed "White Mouse" by the Gestapo for her ability to evade capture. As an SOE agent, she commanded 7,000 resistance fighters during the liberation of France.

STRATEGIC FORCES

The United States also had its own secret army under the Office of Strategic Services. Masterminded by General "Wild Bill"

On November 25, 1942, SOE officers and 150 Greek partisans sabotaged the Gorgopotamos railway bridge in Greece. Early successes like this showed that clandestine operations were worth the risks.

Donovan, the OSS came to Britain in 1942. Using SOE bases, it trained and equipped Free French agents and French-speaking Americans to infiltrate occupied France and support the D-Day invasion. By 1944, the French resistance numbered in the tens of thousands. The OSS organized weapon and supply drops, intelligence gathering, and sabotage behind enemy lines.

A French resistance fighter

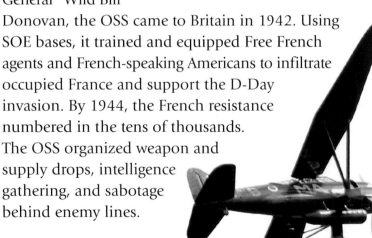

Agents in occupied France were often "exfiltrated" back to Britain, using Lysander aircraft.

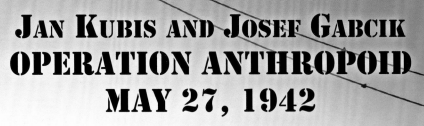

Jan Kubis and Josef Gabcik
OPERATION ANTHROPOID
MAY 27, 1942

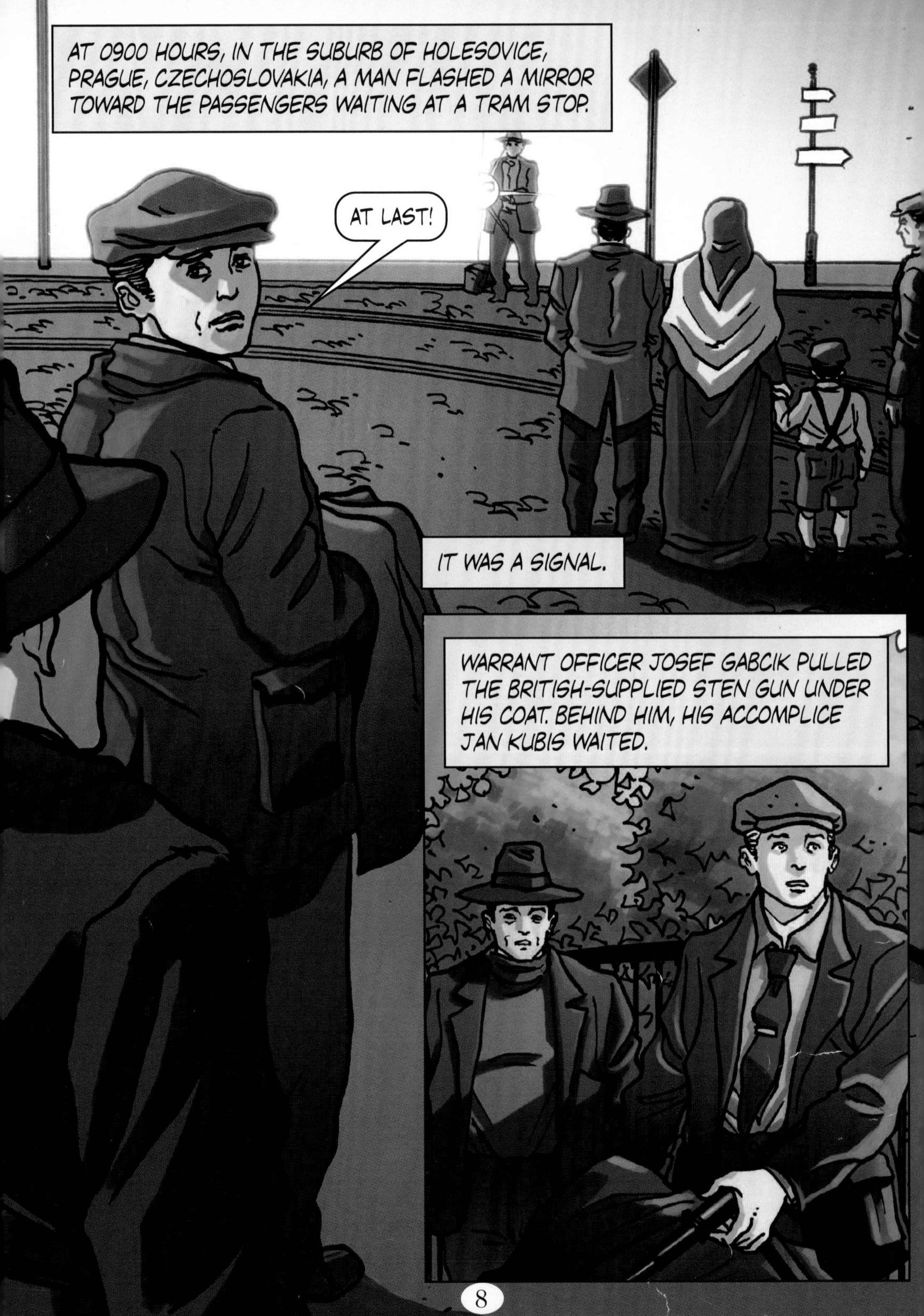

AT 0900 HOURS, IN THE SUBURB OF HOLESOVICE, PRAGUE, CZECHOSLOVAKIA, A MAN FLASHED A MIRROR TOWARD THE PASSENGERS WAITING AT A TRAM STOP.
AT LAST!
IT WAS A SIGNAL.
WARRANT OFFICER JOSEF GABCIK PULLED THE BRITISH-SUPPLIED STEN GUN UNDER HIS COAT. BEHIND HIM, HIS ACCOMPLICE JAN KUBIS WAITED.

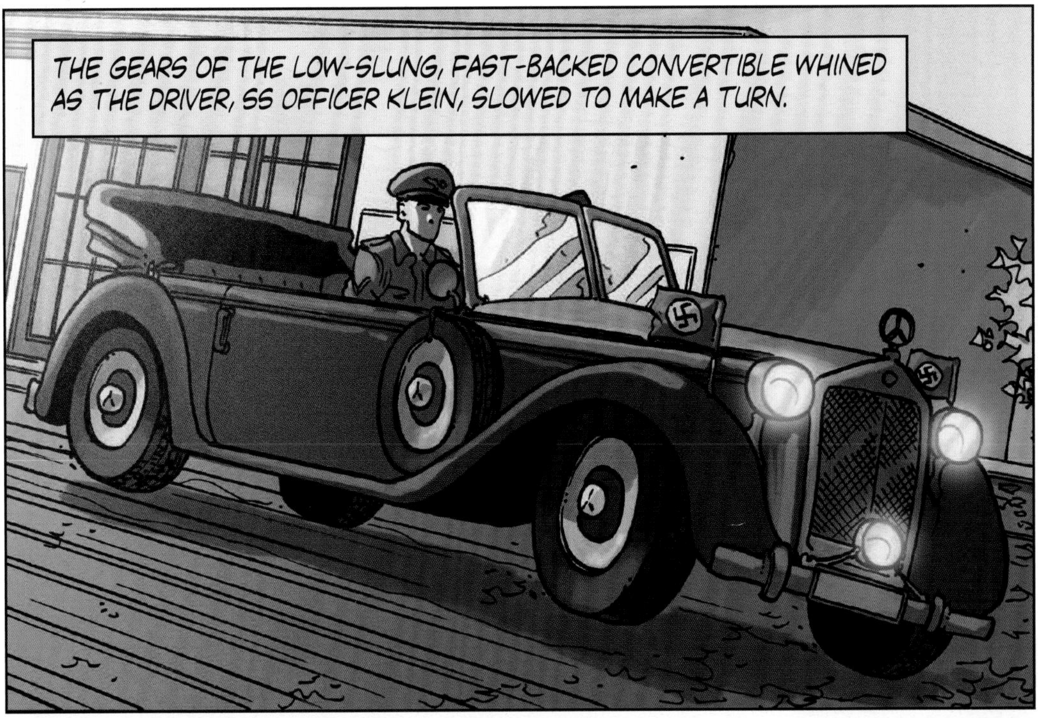
THE GEARS OF THE LOW-SLUNG, FAST-BACKED CONVERTIBLE WHINED AS THE DRIVER, SS OFFICER KLEIN, SLOWED TO MAKE A TURN.

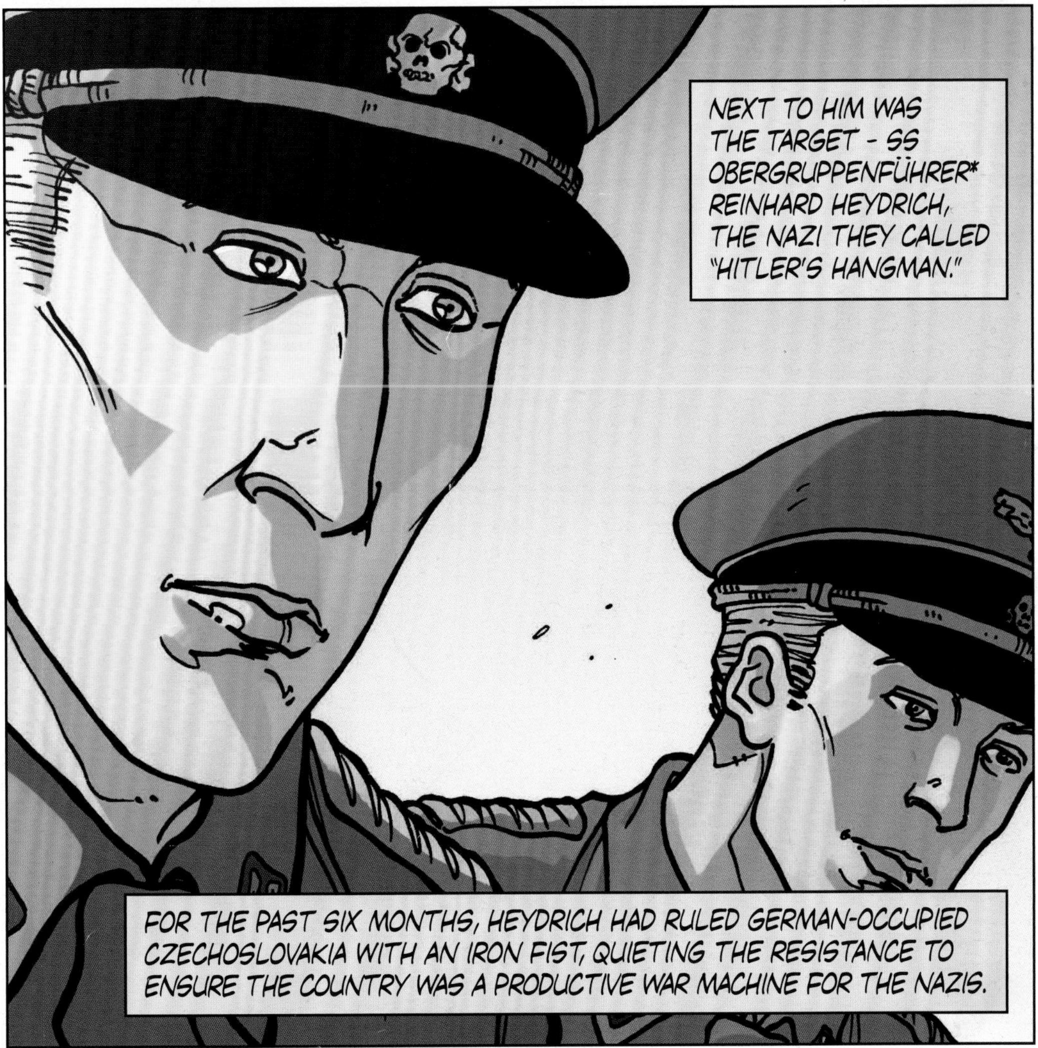
NEXT TO HIM WAS THE TARGET - SS OBERGRUPPENFÜHRER* REINHARD HEYDRICH, THE NAZI THEY CALLED "HITLER'S HANGMAN."
FOR THE PAST SIX MONTHS, HEYDRICH HAD RULED GERMAN-OCCUPIED CZECHOSLOVAKIA WITH AN IRON FIST, QUIETING THE RESISTANCE TO ENSURE THE COUNTRY WAS A PRODUCTIVE WAR MACHINE FOR THE NAZIS.

*UPPER GROUP LEADER

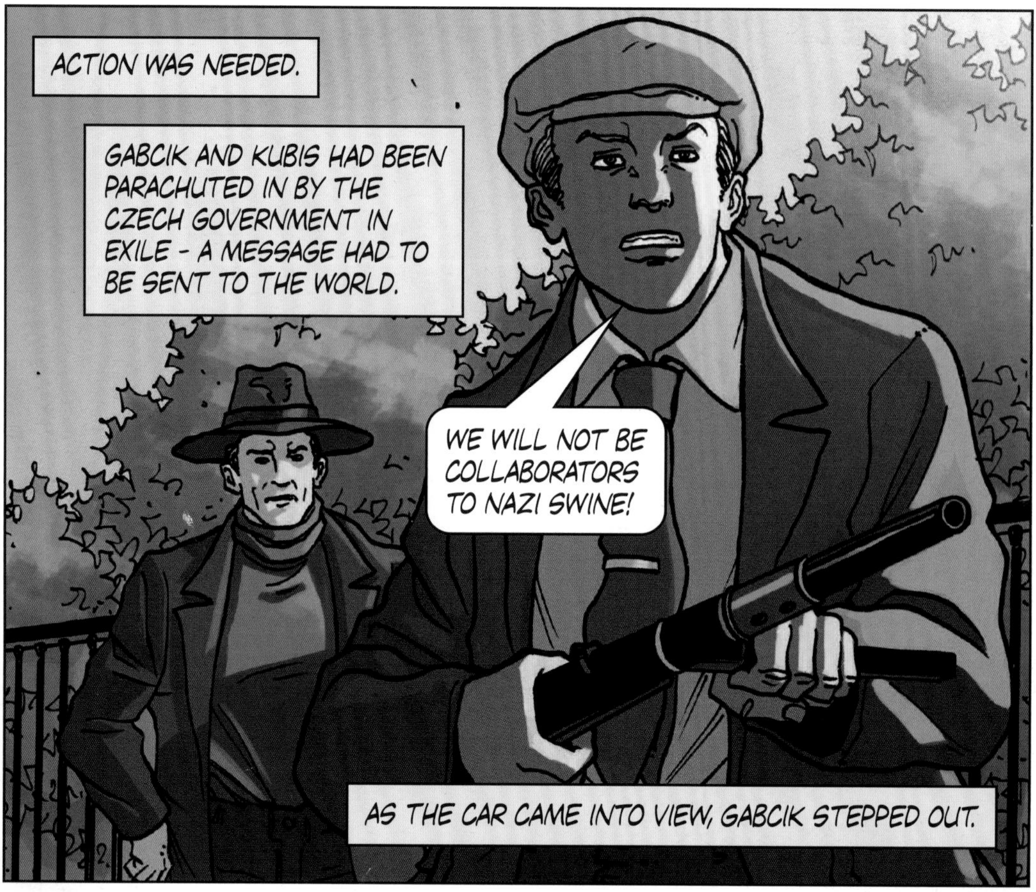
ACTION WAS NEEDED.
GABCIK AND KUBIS HAD BEEN PARACHUTED IN BY THE CZECH GOVERNMENT IN EXILE - A MESSAGE HAD TO BE SENT TO THE WORLD.
WE WILL NOT BE COLLABORATORS TO NAZI SWINE!
AS THE CAR CAME INTO VIEW, GABCIK STEPPED OUT.

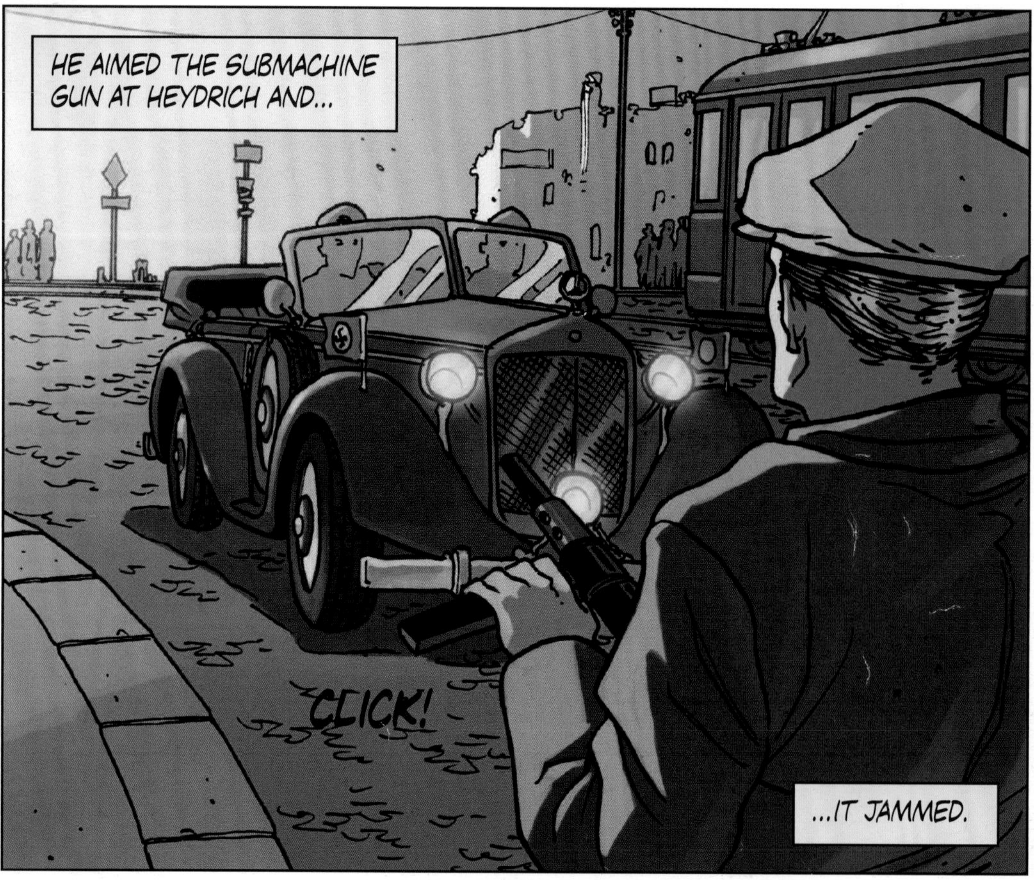
HE AIMED THE SUBMACHINE GUN AT HEYDRICH AND...
CLICK!
...IT JAMMED.

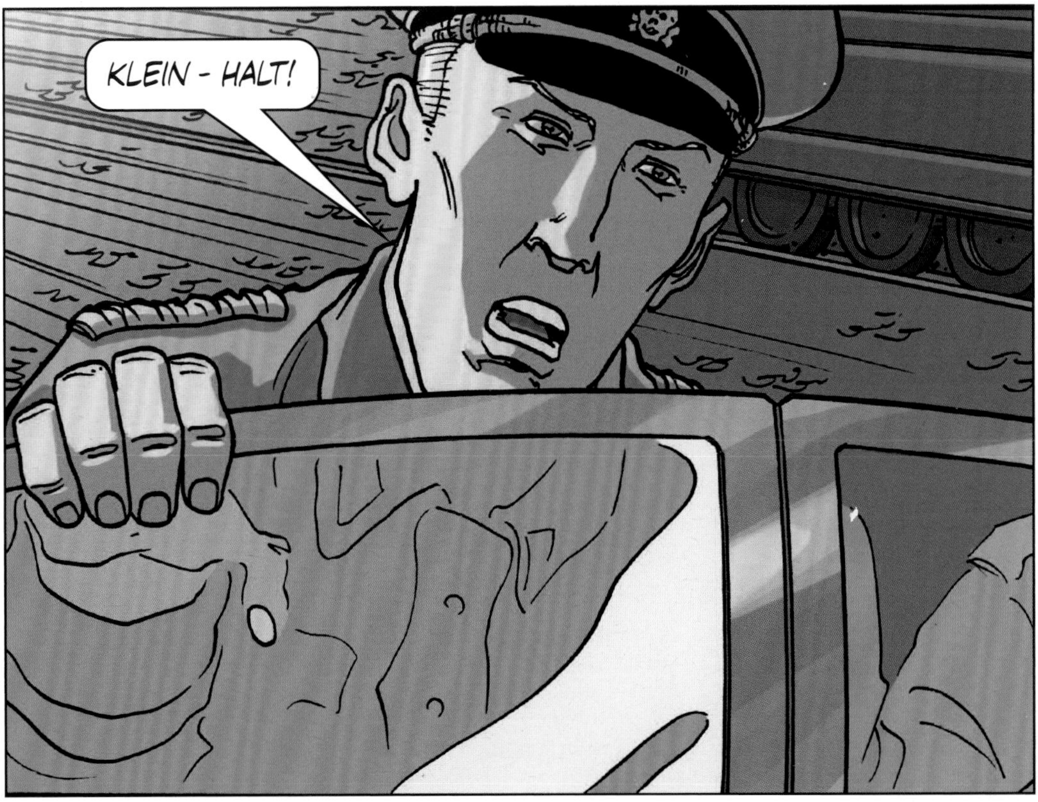
KLEIN - HALT!

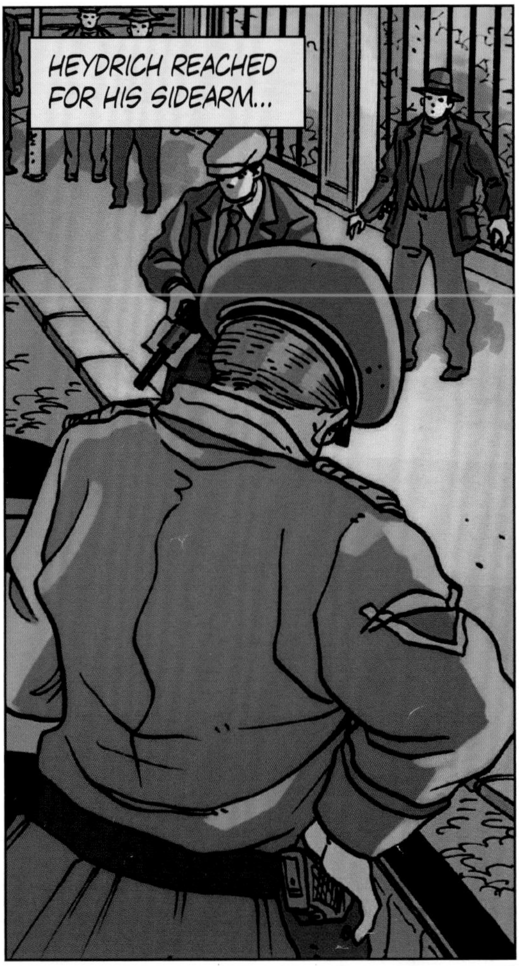
HEYDRICH REACHED FOR HIS SIDEARM...

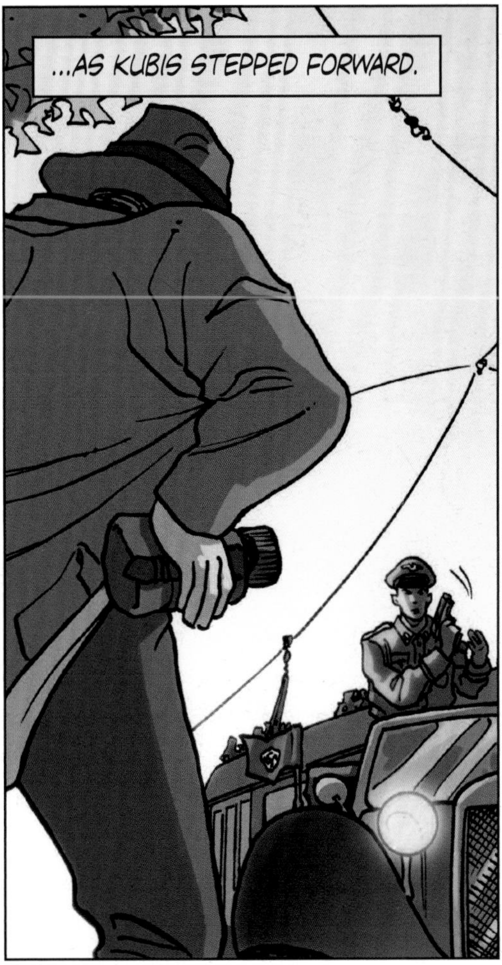
...AS KUBIS STEPPED FORWARD.

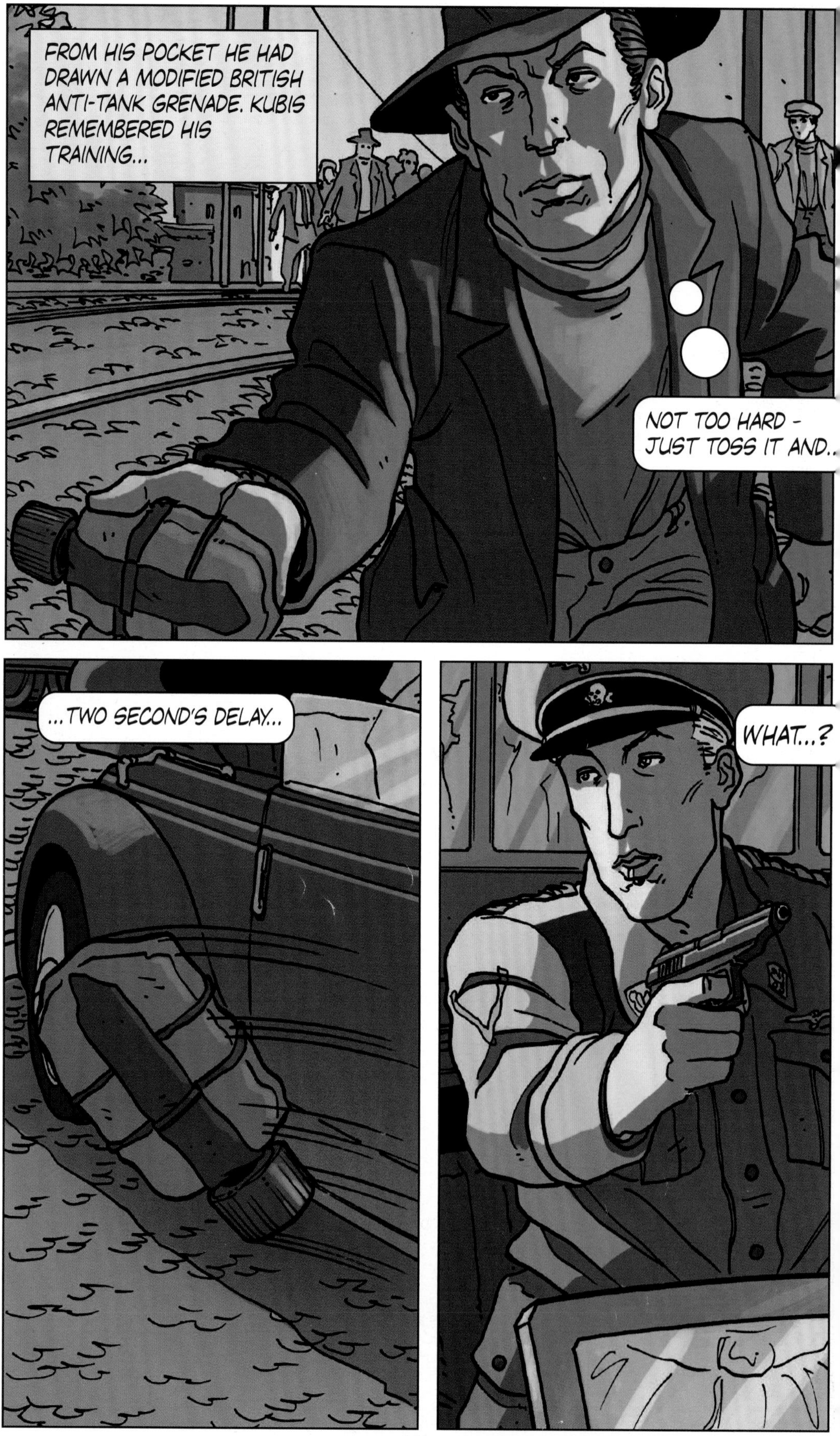

FROM HIS POCKET HE HAD DRAWN A MODIFIED BRITISH ANTI-TANK GRENADE. KUBIS REMEMBERED HIS TRAINING...
NOT TOO HARD - JUST TOSS IT AND..
...TWO SECOND'S DELAY...
WHAT...?

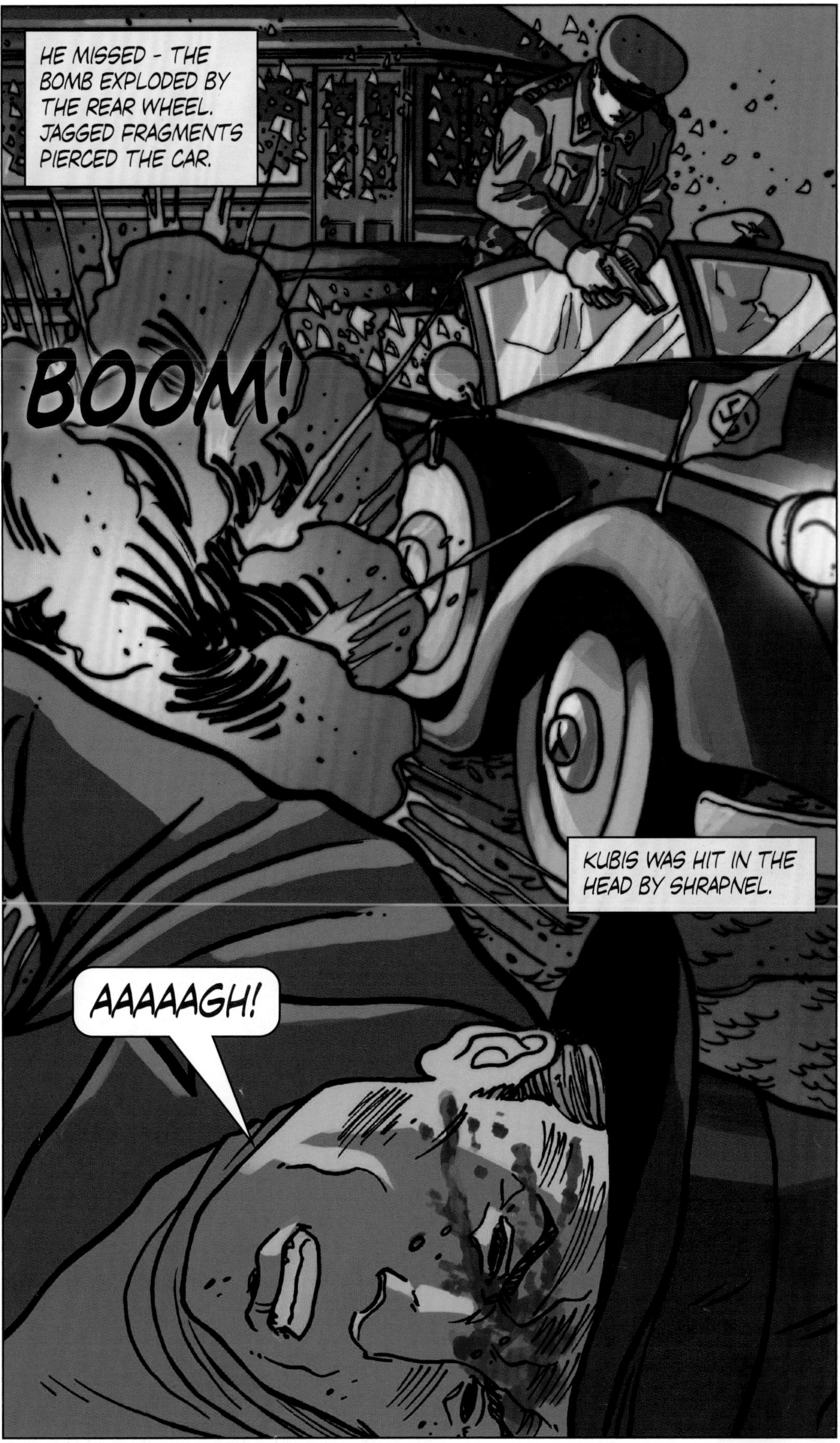
HE MISSED - THE BOMB EXPLODED BY THE REAR WHEEL. JAGGED FRAGMENTS PIERCED THE CAR.
BOOM!
KUBIS WAS HIT IN THE HEAD BY SHRAPNEL.
AAAAAGH!

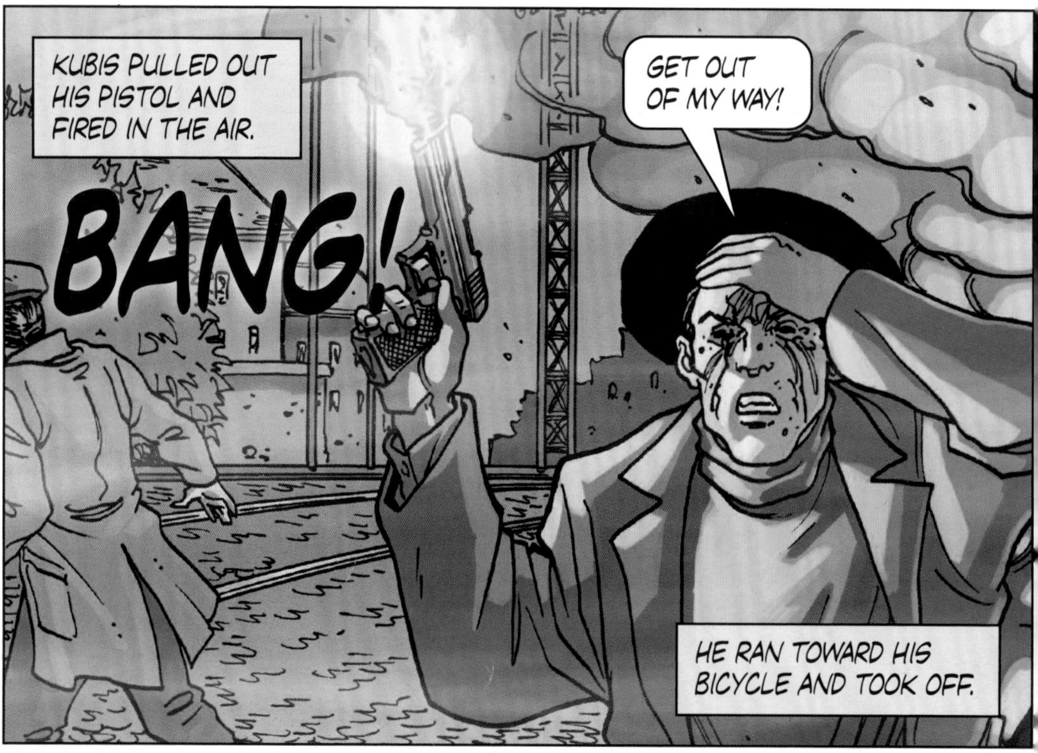
KUBIS PULLED OUT HIS PISTOL AND FIRED IN THE AIR.
BANG!
GET OUT OF MY WAY!
HE RAN TOWARD HIS BICYCLE AND TOOK OFF.

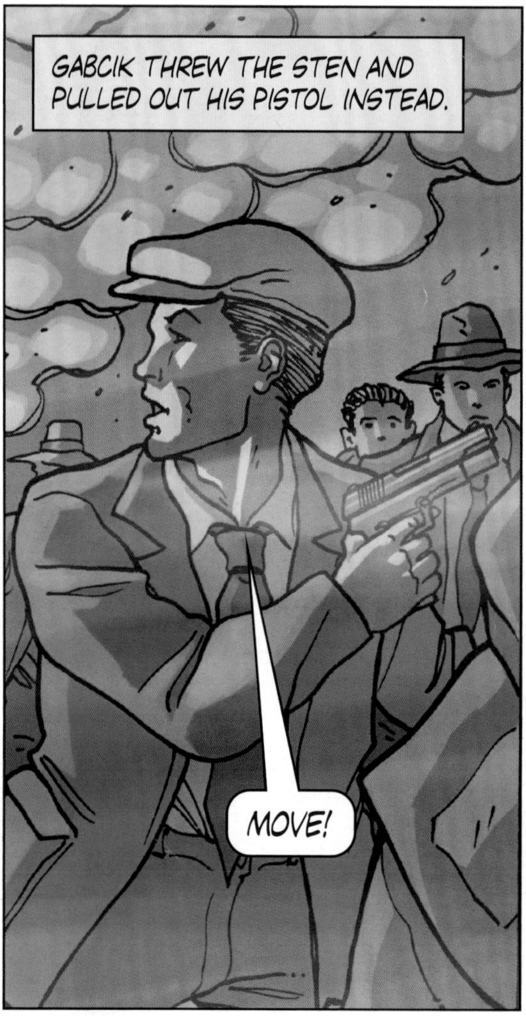
GABCIK THREW THE STEN AND PULLED OUT HIS PISTOL INSTEAD.
MOVE!

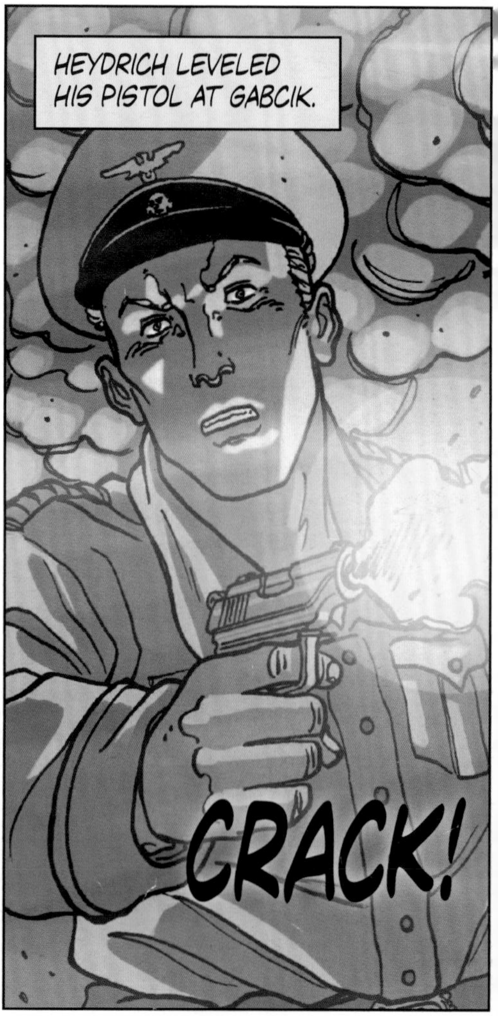
HEYDRICH LEVELED HIS PISTOL AT GABCIK.
CRACK!

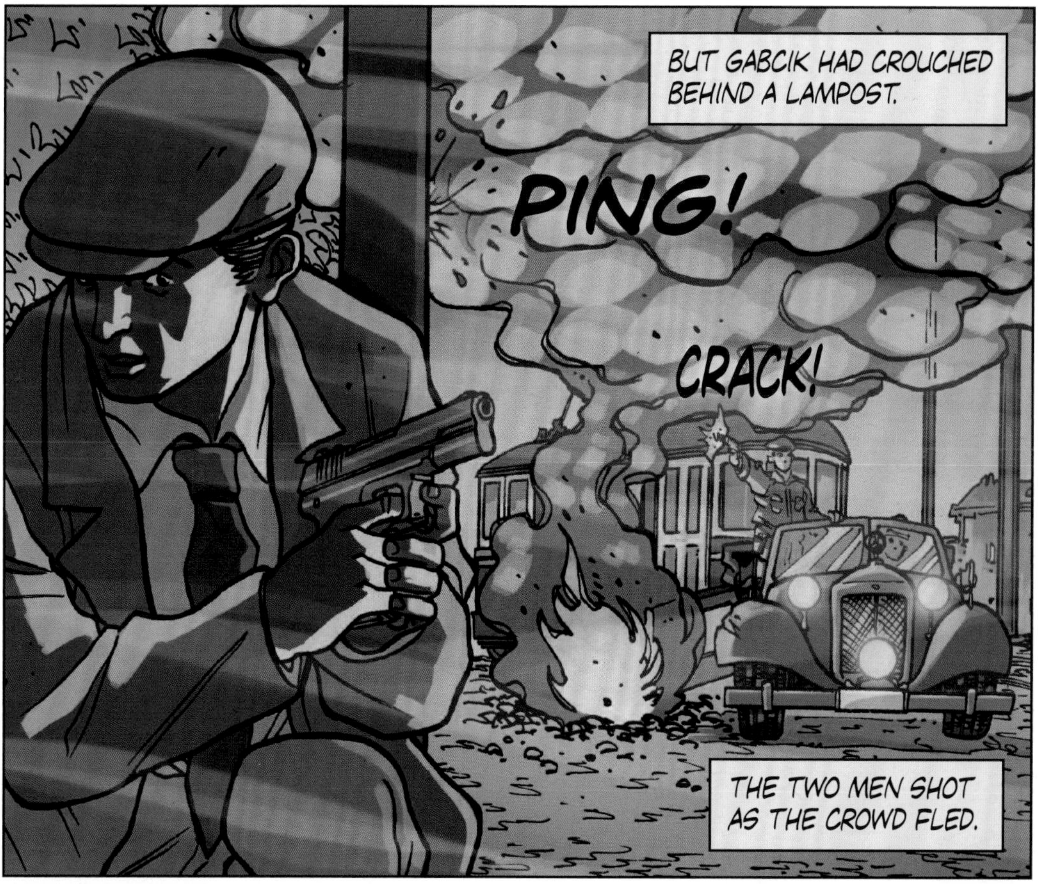
BUT GABCIK HAD CROUCHED BEHIND A LAMPOST.
PING!
CRACK!
THE TWO MEN SHOT AS THE CROWD FLED.

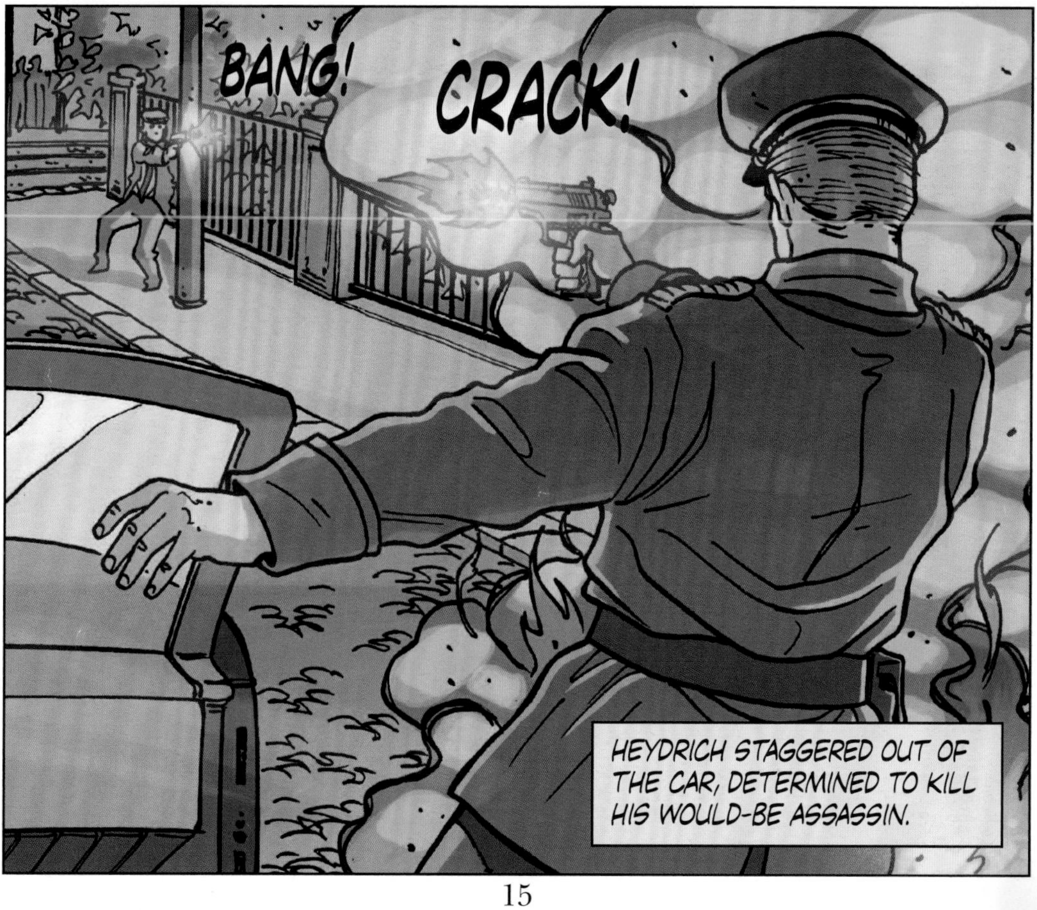
BANG!
CRACK!
HEYDRICH STAGGERED OUT OF THE CAR, DETERMINED TO KILL HIS WOULD-BE ASSASSIN.

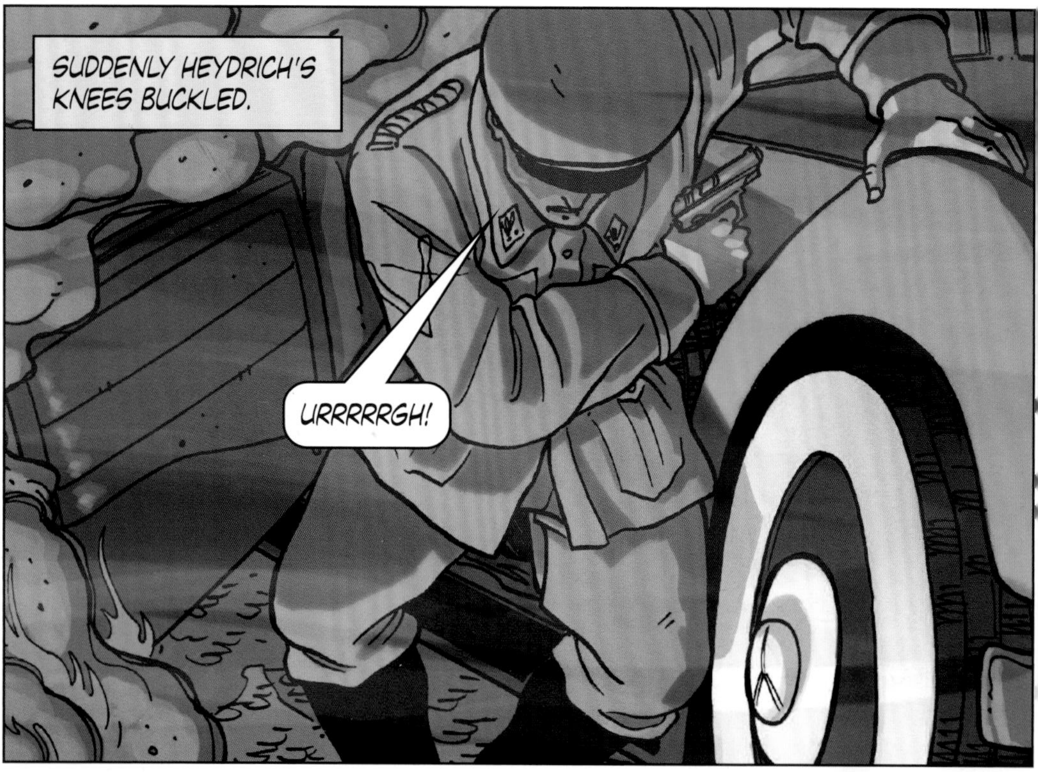
SUDDENLY HEYDRICH'S KNEES BUCKLED.
URRRRRGH!

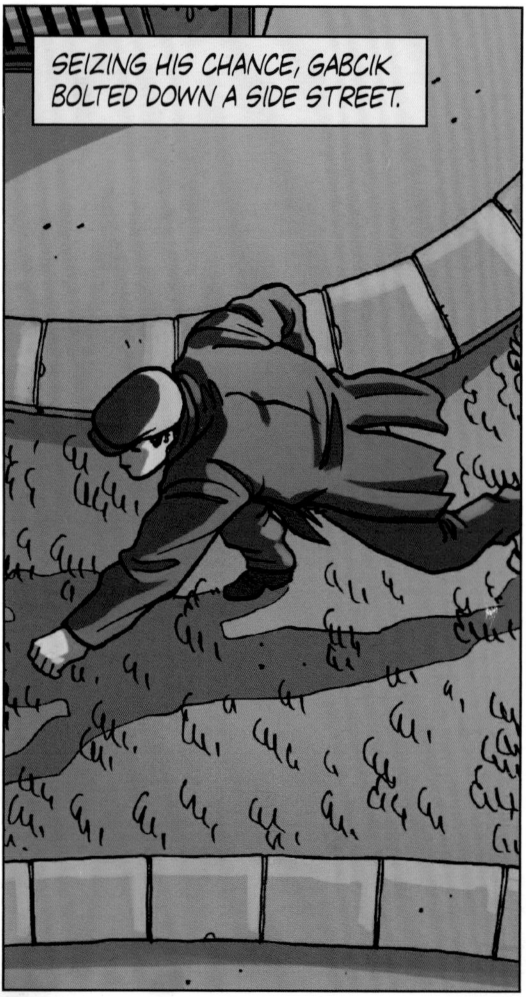
SEIZING HIS CHANCE, GABCIK BOLTED DOWN A SIDE STREET.

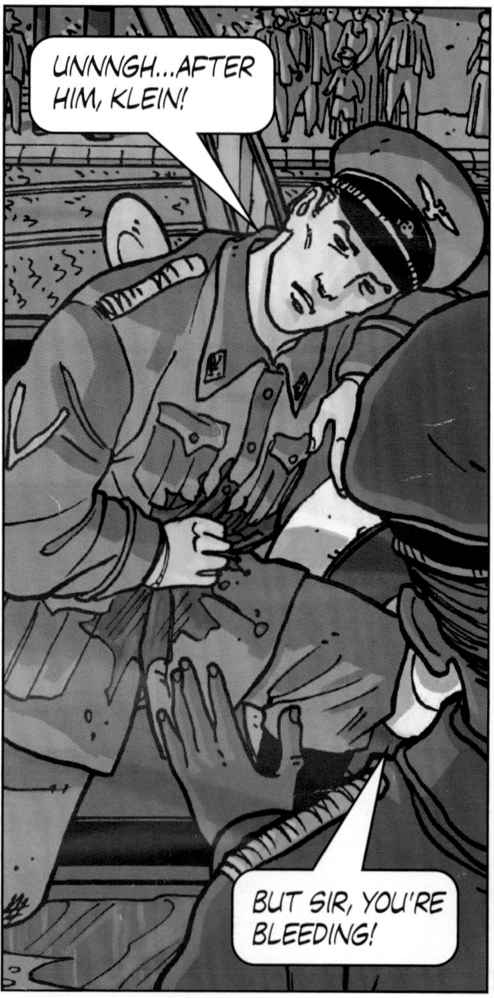
UNNNGH...AFTER HIM, KLEIN!
BUT SIR, YOU'RE BLEEDING!

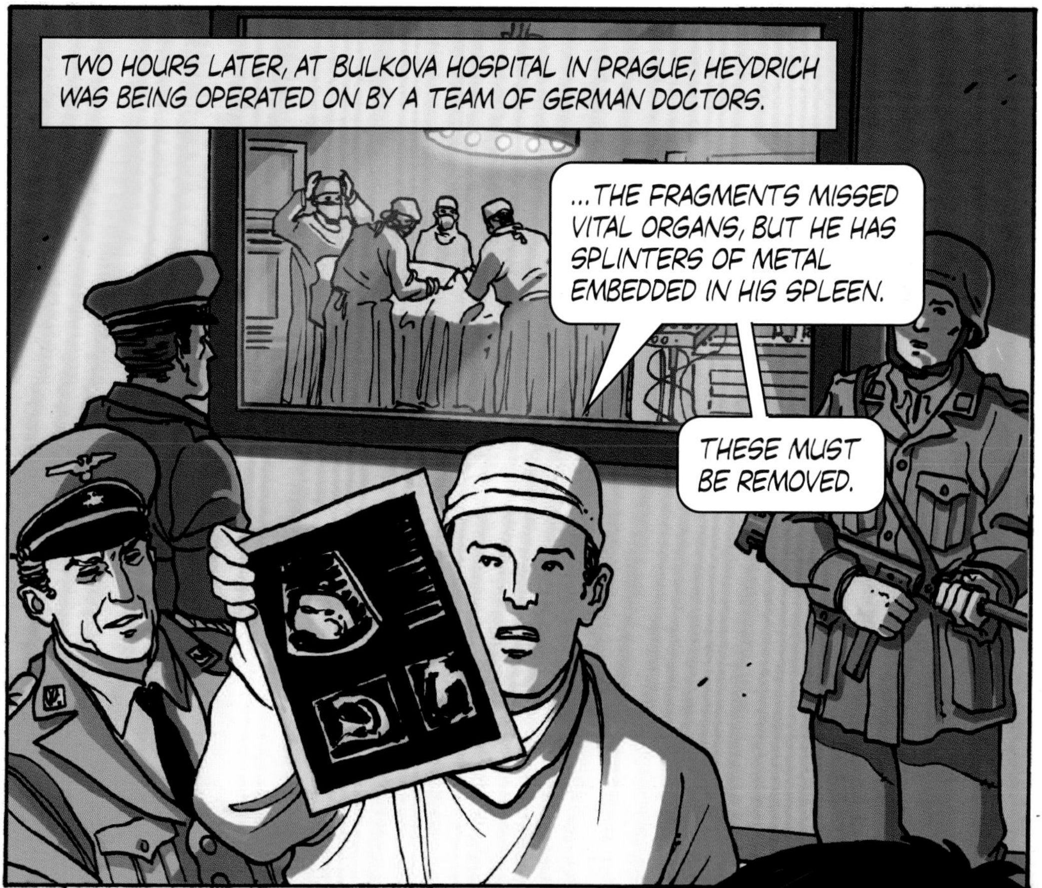
TWO HOURS LATER, AT BULKOVA HOSPITAL IN PRAGUE, HEYDRICH WAS BEING OPERATED ON BY A TEAM OF GERMAN DOCTORS.
...THE FRAGMENTS MISSED VITAL ORGANS, BUT HE HAS SPLINTERS OF METAL EMBEDDED IN HIS SPLEEN.
THESE MUST BE REMOVED.

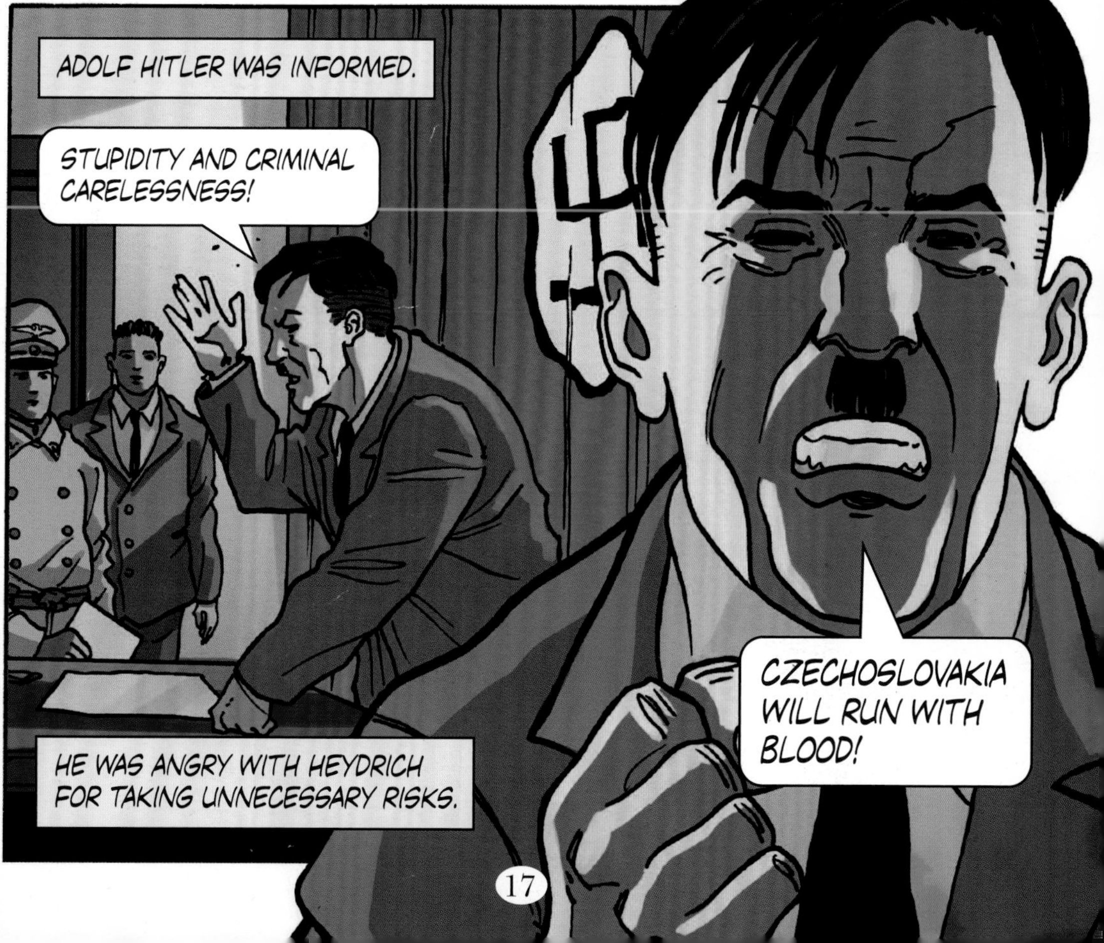
ADOLF HITLER WAS INFORMED.
STUPIDITY AND CRIMINAL CARELESSNESS!
CZECHOSLOVAKIA WILL RUN WITH BLOOD!
HE WAS ANGRY WITH HEYDRICH FOR TAKING UNNECESSARY RISKS.

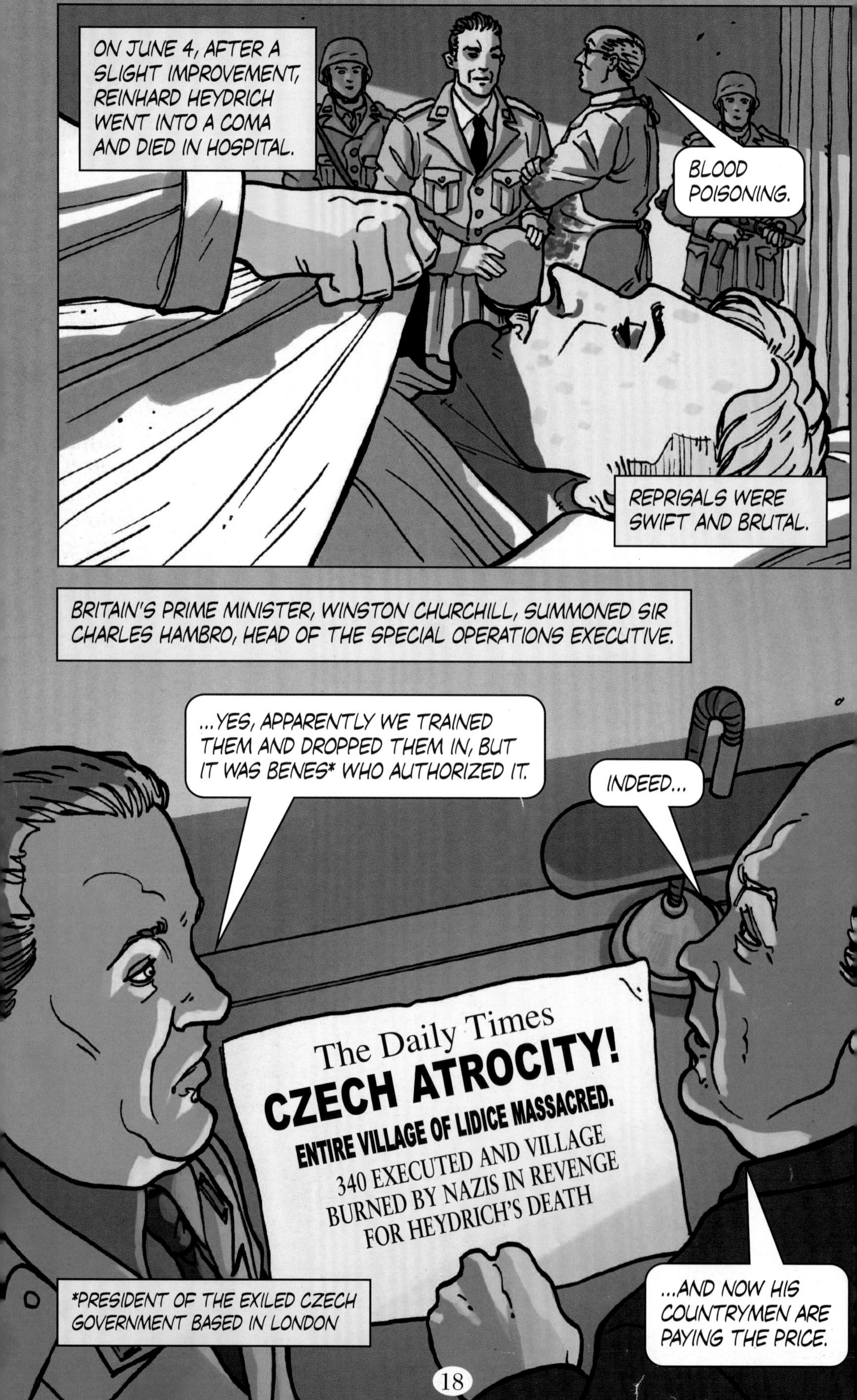
ON JUNE 4, AFTER A SLIGHT IMPROVEMENT, REINHARD HEYDRICH WENT INTO A COMA AND DIED IN HOSPITAL.
BLOOD POISONING.
REPRISALS WERE SWIFT AND BRUTAL.
BRITAIN'S PRIME MINISTER, WINSTON CHURCHILL, SUMMONED SIR CHARLES HAMBRO, HEAD OF THE SPECIAL OPERATIONS EXECUTIVE.
...YES, APPARENTLY WE TRAINED THEM AND DROPPED THEM IN, BUT IT WAS BENES* WHO AUTHORIZED IT.
INDEED...
The Daily Times
CZECH ATROCITY!
ENTIRE VILLAGE OF LIDICE MASSACRED.
340 EXECUTED AND VILLAGE BURNED BY NAZIS IN REVENGE FOR HEYDRICH'S DEATH
...AND NOW HIS COUNTRYMEN ARE PAYING THE PRICE.
*PRESIDENT OF THE EXILED CZECH GOVERNMENT BASED IN LONDON

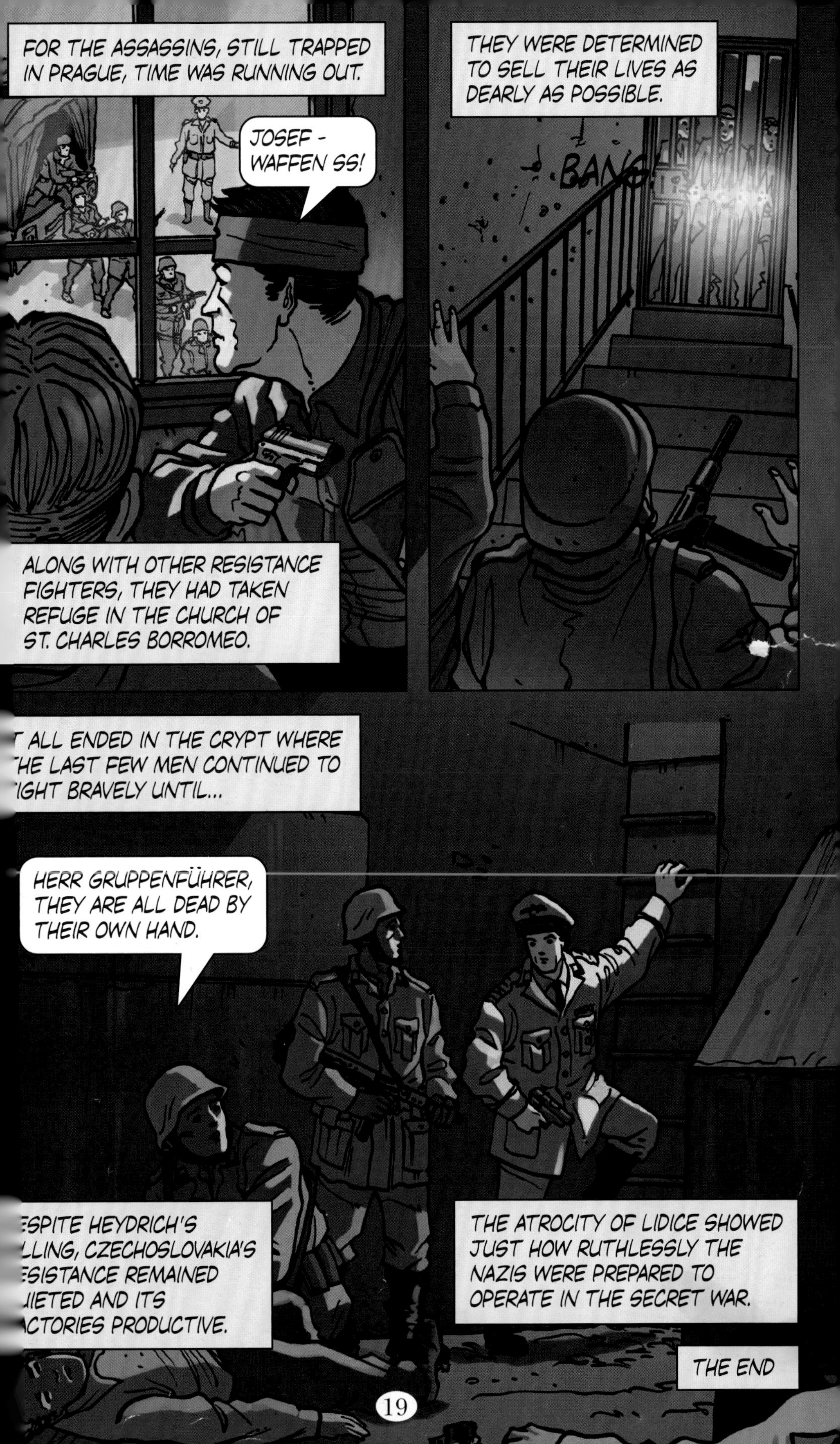
FOR THE ASSASSINS, STILL TRAPPED IN PRAGUE, TIME WAS RUNNING OUT.
JOSEF - WAFFEN SS!
ALONG WITH OTHER RESISTANCE FIGHTERS, THEY HAD TAKEN REFUGE IN THE CHURCH OF ST. CHARLES BORROMEO.
THEY WERE DETERMINED TO SELL THEIR LIVES AS DEARLY AS POSSIBLE.
BANG!
ALL ENDED IN THE CRYPT WHERE HE LAST FEW MEN CONTINUED TO IGHT BRAVELY UNTIL...
HERR GRUPPENFÜHRER, THEY ARE ALL DEAD BY THEIR OWN HAND.
ESPITE HEYDRICH'S LLING, CZECHOSLOVAKIA'S ESISTANCE REMAINED IETED AND ITS ACTORIES PRODUCTIVE.
THE ATROCITY OF LIDICE SHOWED JUST HOW RUTHLESSLY THE NAZIS WERE PREPARED TO OPERATE IN THE SECRET WAR.
THE END

Benjamin Cowburn
SOE—OPERATION TINKER
APRIL 1943

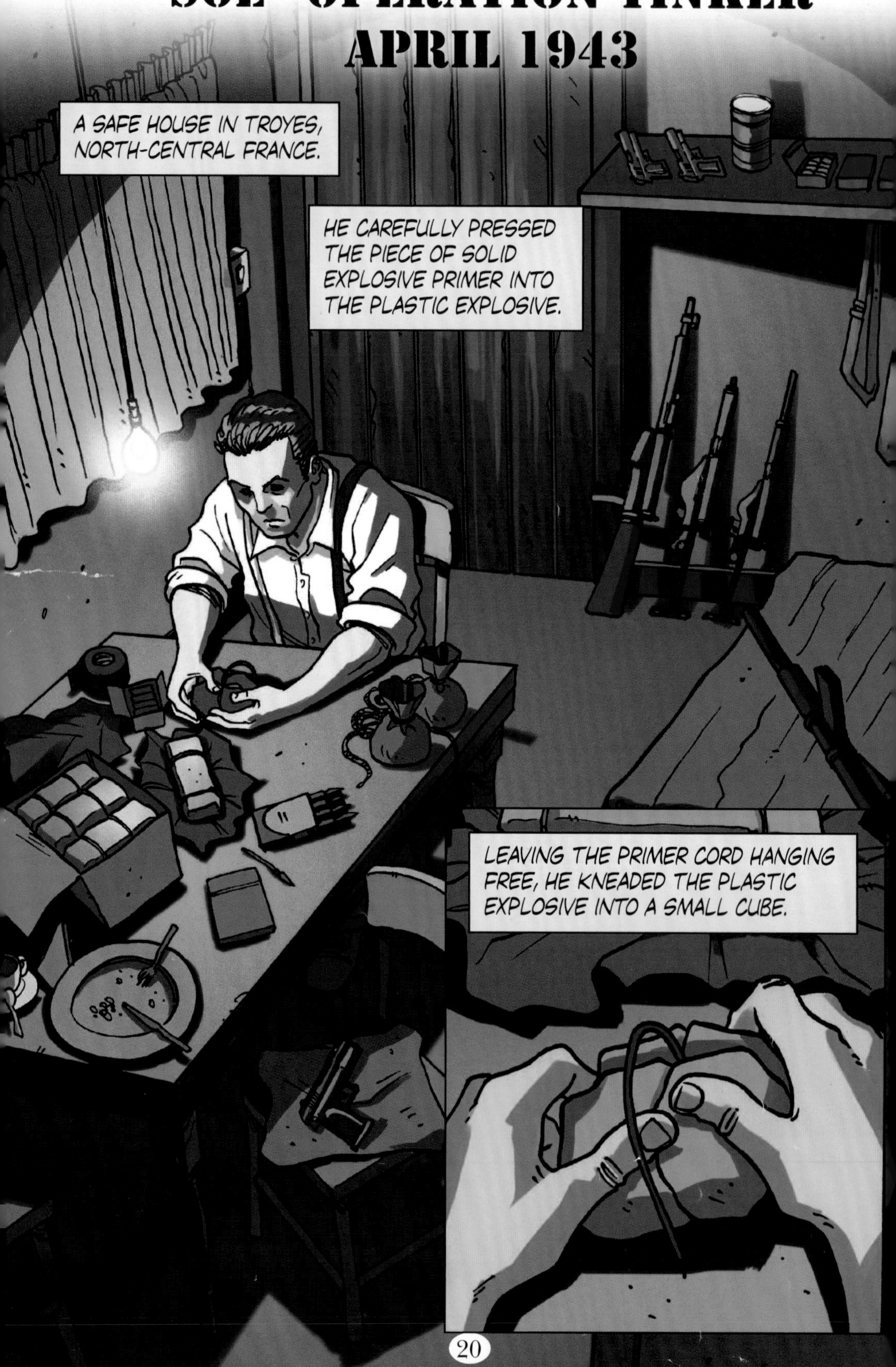
A SAFE HOUSE IN TROYES, NORTH-CENTRAL FRANCE.
HE CAREFULLY PRESSED THE PIECE OF SOLID EXPLOSIVE PRIMER INTO THE PLASTIC EXPLOSIVE.
LEAVING THE PRIMER CORD HANGING FREE, HE KNEADED THE PLASTIC EXPLOSIVE INTO A SMALL CUBE.

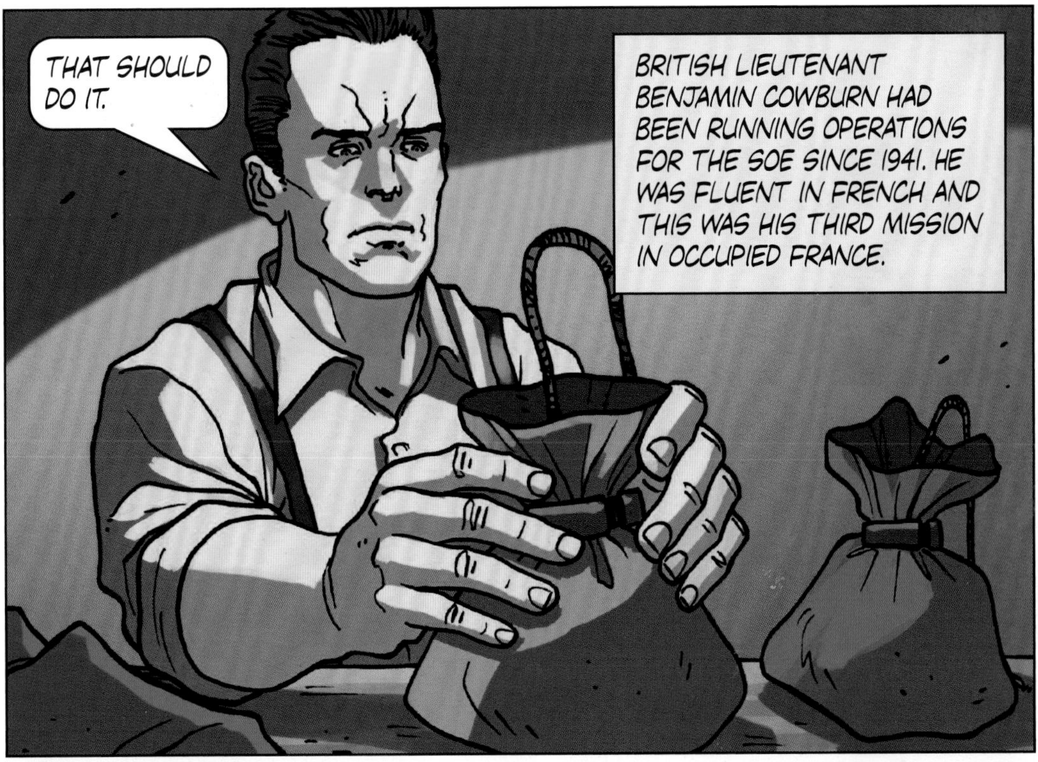
THAT SHOULD DO IT.
BRITISH LIEUTENANT BENJAMIN COWBURN HAD BEEN RUNNING OPERATIONS FOR THE SOE SINCE 1941. HE WAS FLUENT IN FRENCH AND THIS WAS HIS THIRD MISSION IN OCCUPIED FRANCE.

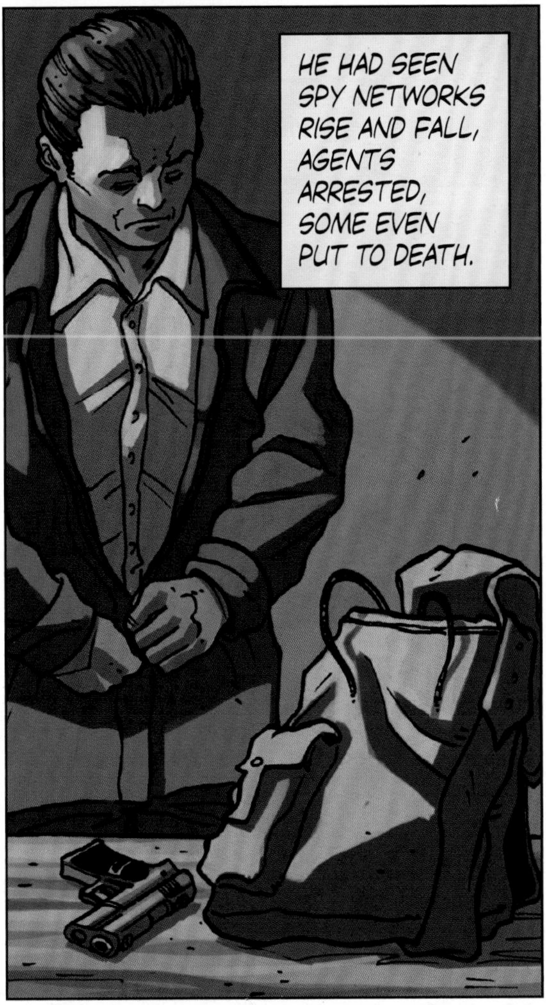
HE HAD SEEN SPY NETWORKS RISE AND FALL, AGENTS ARRESTED, SOME EVEN PUT TO DEATH.

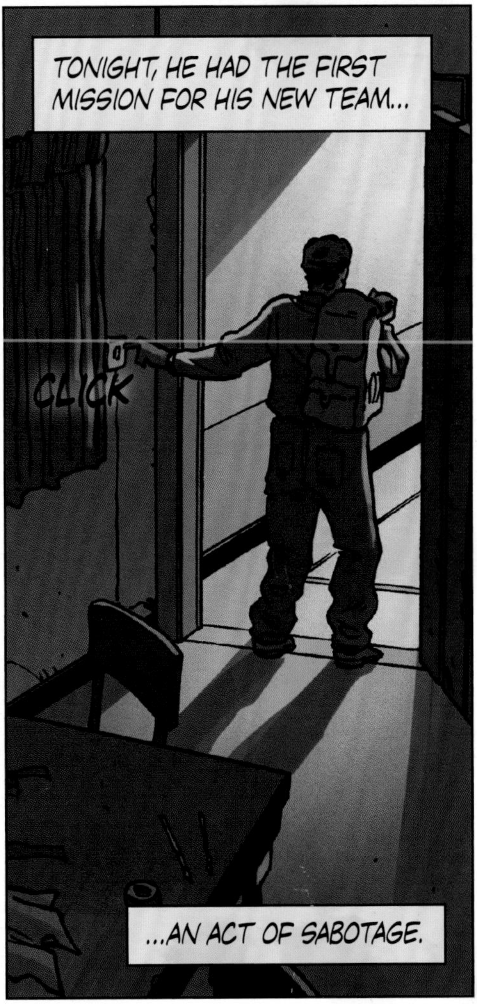
TONIGHT, HE HAD THE FIRST MISSION FOR HIS NEW TEAM...
CLICK
...AN ACT OF SABOTAGE.

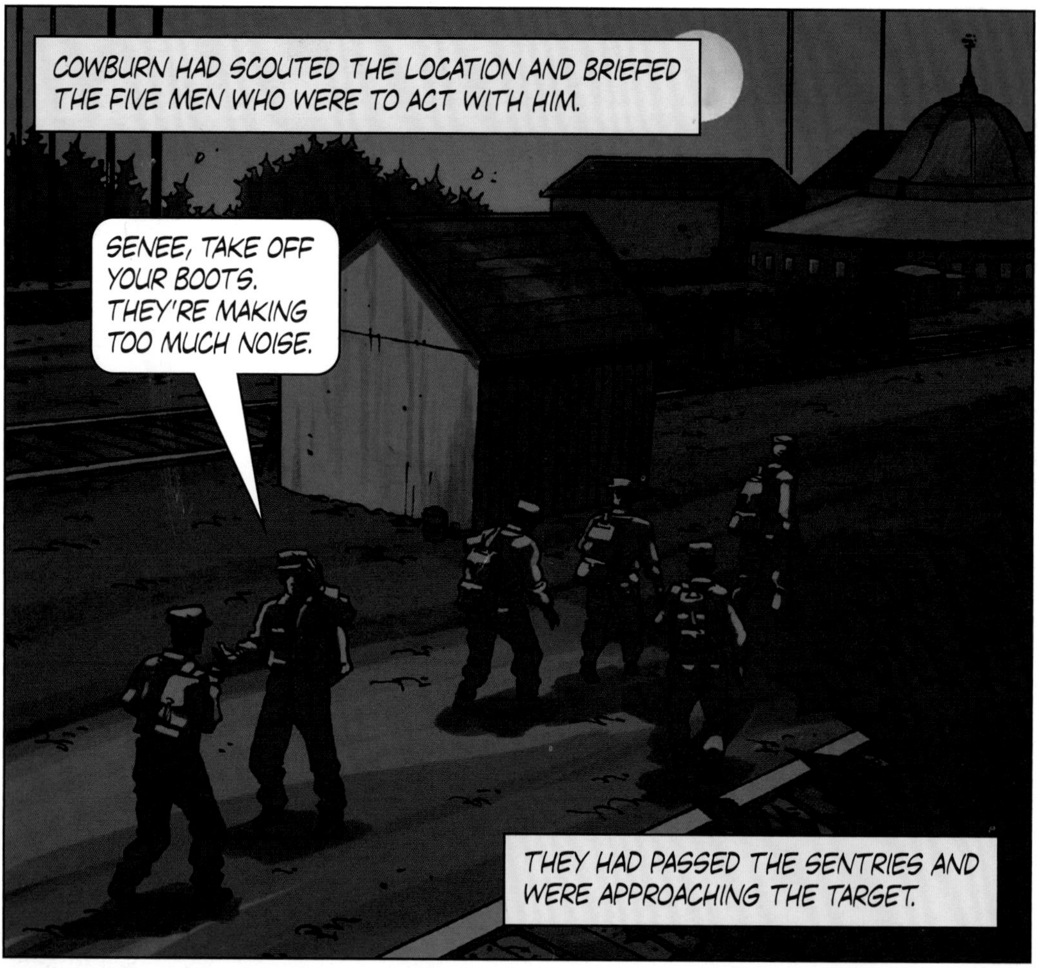
COWBURN HAD SCOUTED THE LOCATION AND BRIEFED THE FIVE MEN WHO WERE TO ACT WITH HIM.
SENEE, TAKE OFF YOUR BOOTS. THEY'RE MAKING TOO MUCH NOISE.
THEY HAD PASSED THE SENTRIES AND WERE APPROACHING THE TARGET.

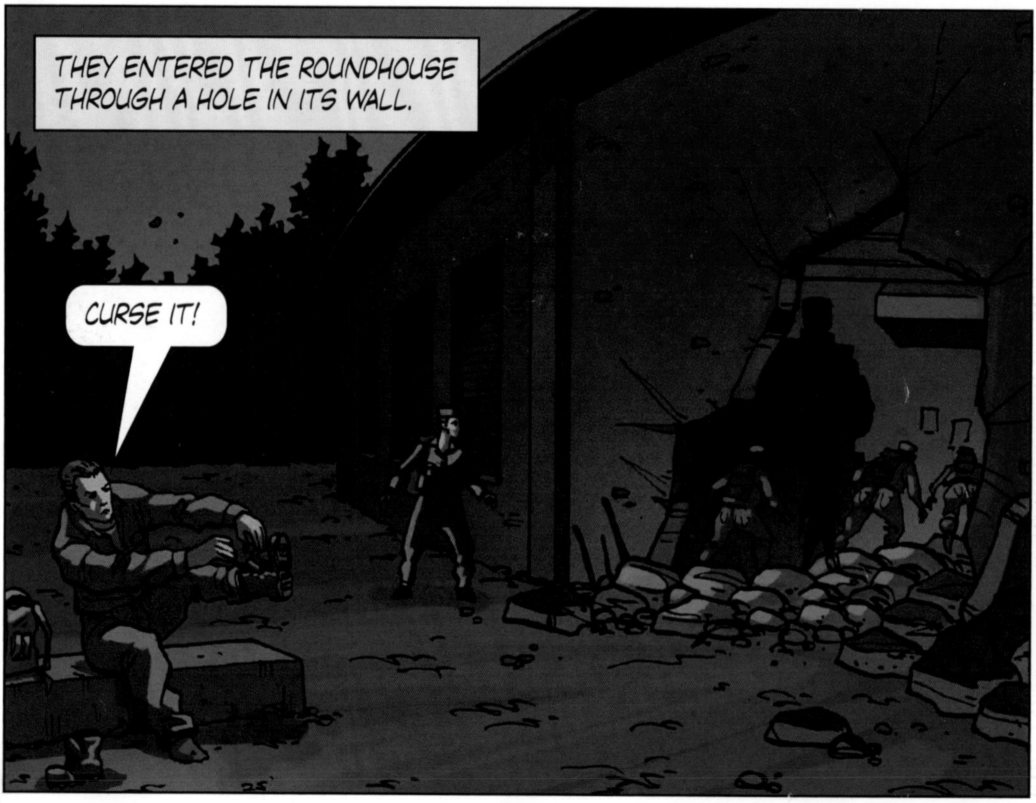
THEY ENTERED THE ROUNDHOUSE THROUGH A HOLE IN ITS WALL.
CURSE IT!

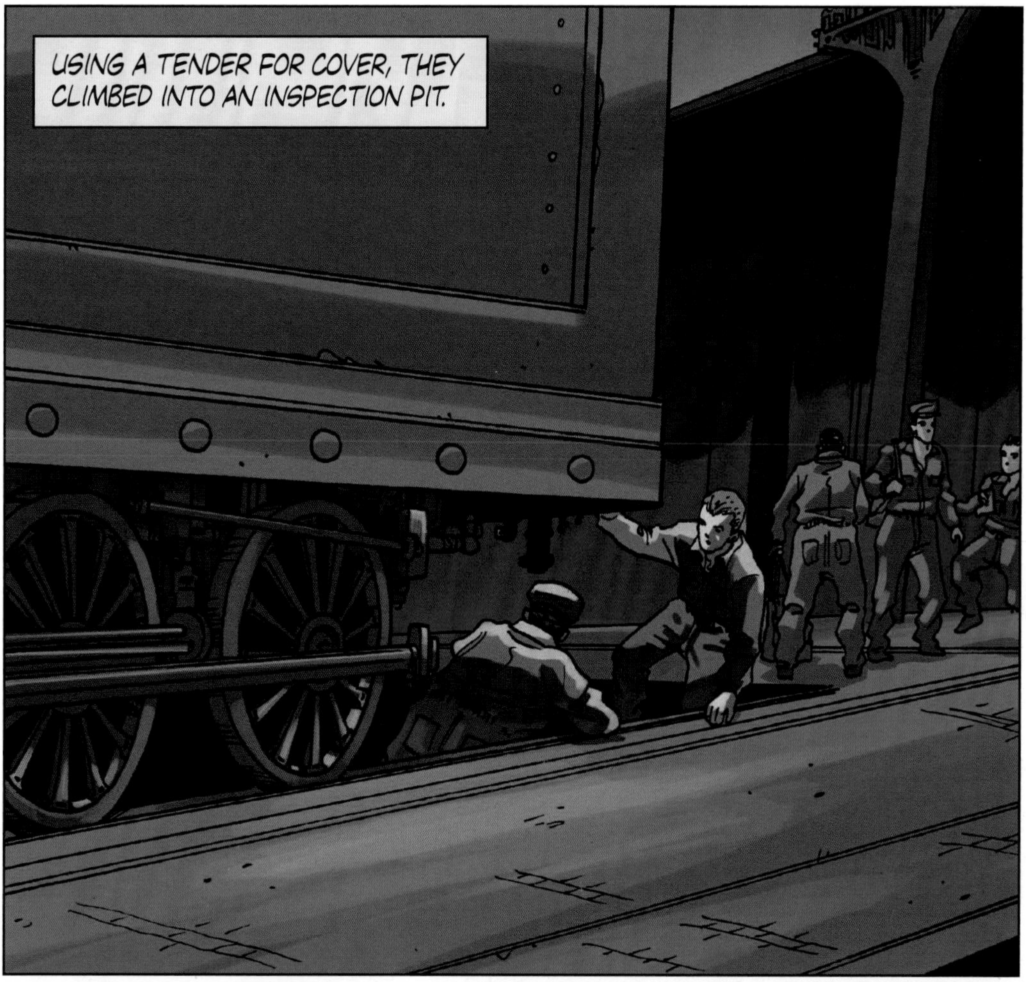
USING A TENDER FOR COVER, THEY CLIMBED INTO AN INSPECTION PIT.

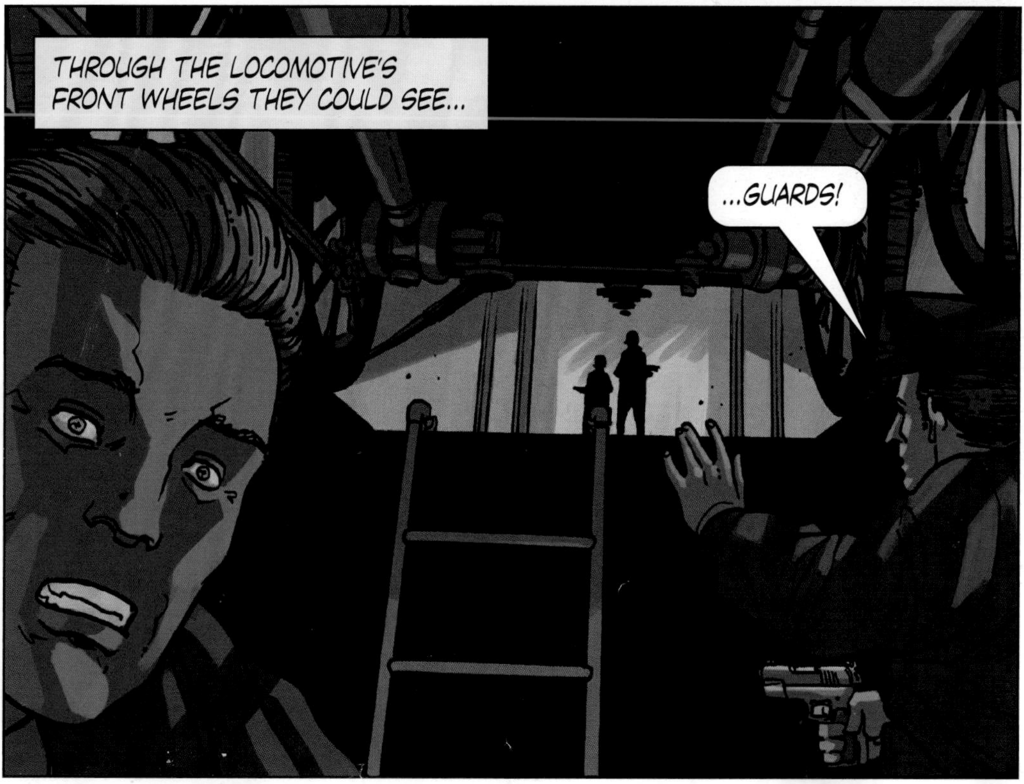
THROUGH THE LOCOMOTIVE'S FRONT WHEELS THEY COULD SEE...
...GUARDS!

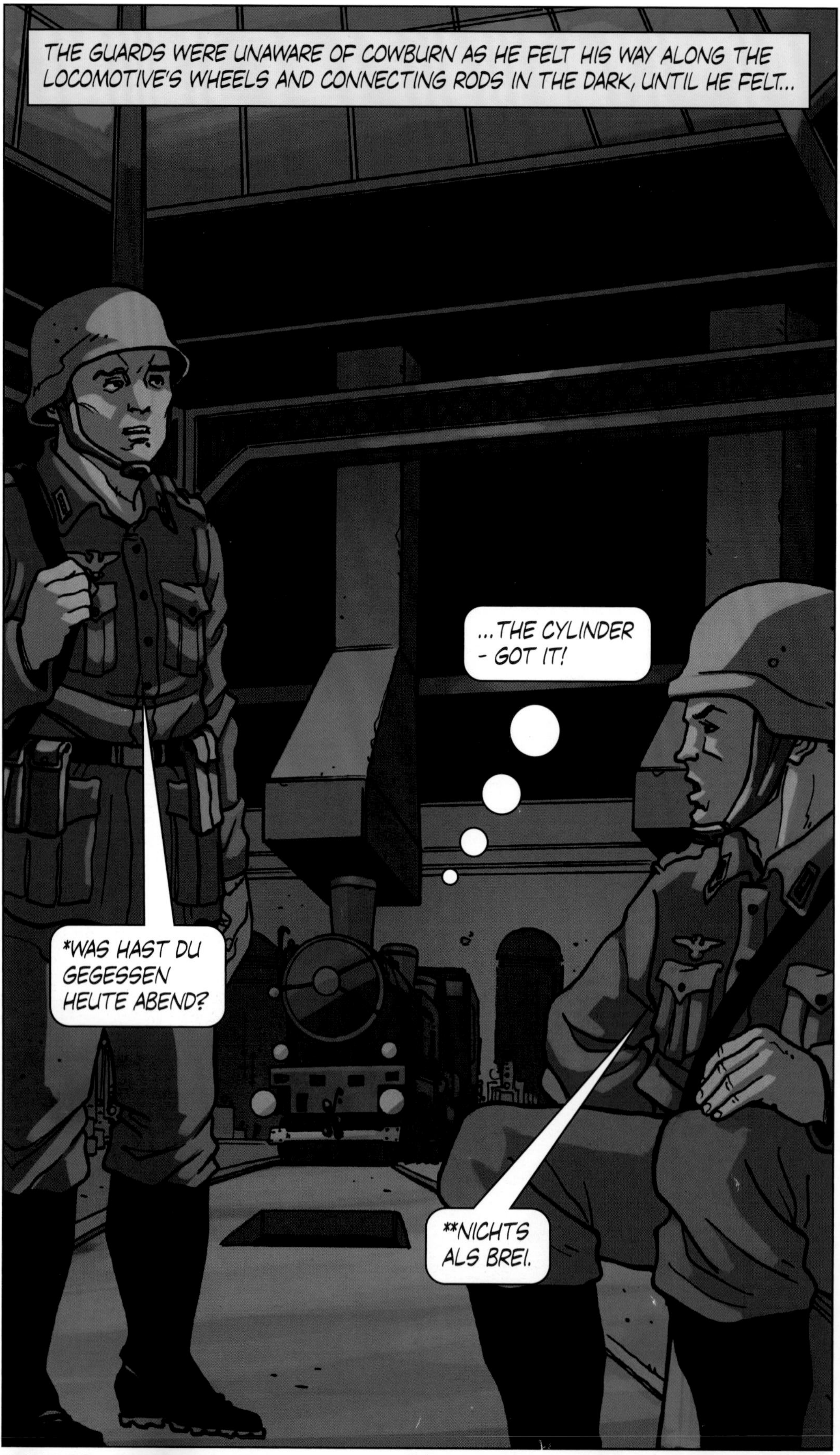
THE GUARDS WERE UNAWARE OF COWBURN AS HE FELT HIS WAY ALONG THE LOCOMOTIVE'S WHEELS AND CONNECTING RODS IN THE DARK, UNTIL HE FELT...
...THE CYLINDER - GOT IT!
*WAS HAST DU GEGESSEN HEUTE ABEND?
**NICHTS ALS BREI.

*WHAT DID YOU EAT TONIGHT?

**NOTHING BUT PORRIDGE.

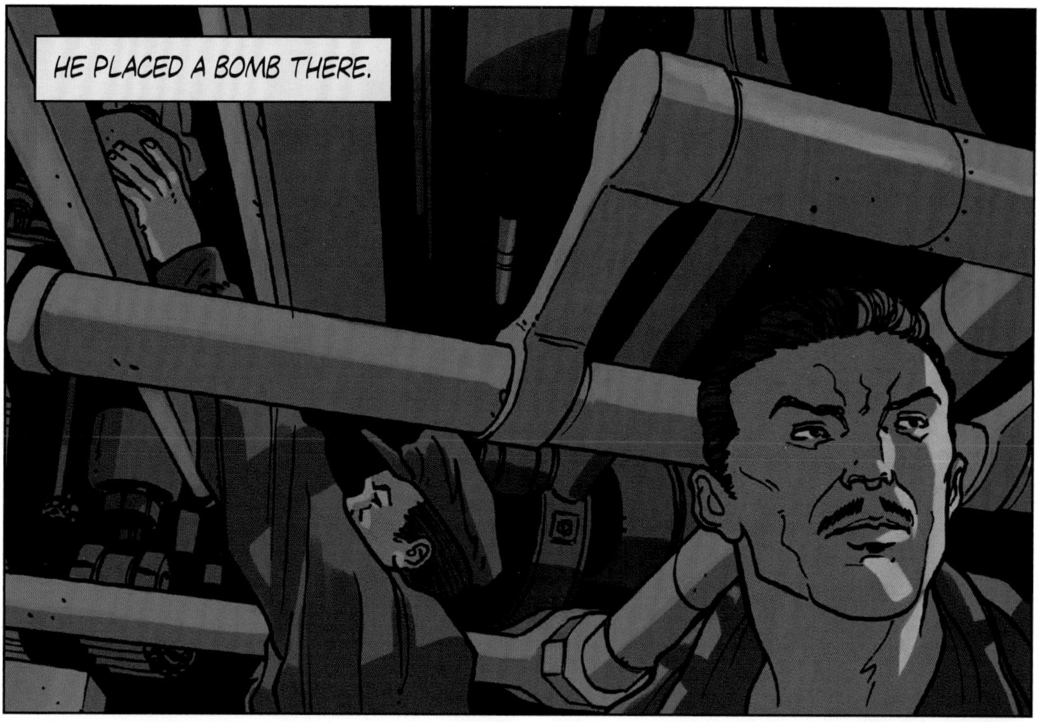
HE PLACED A BOMB THERE.

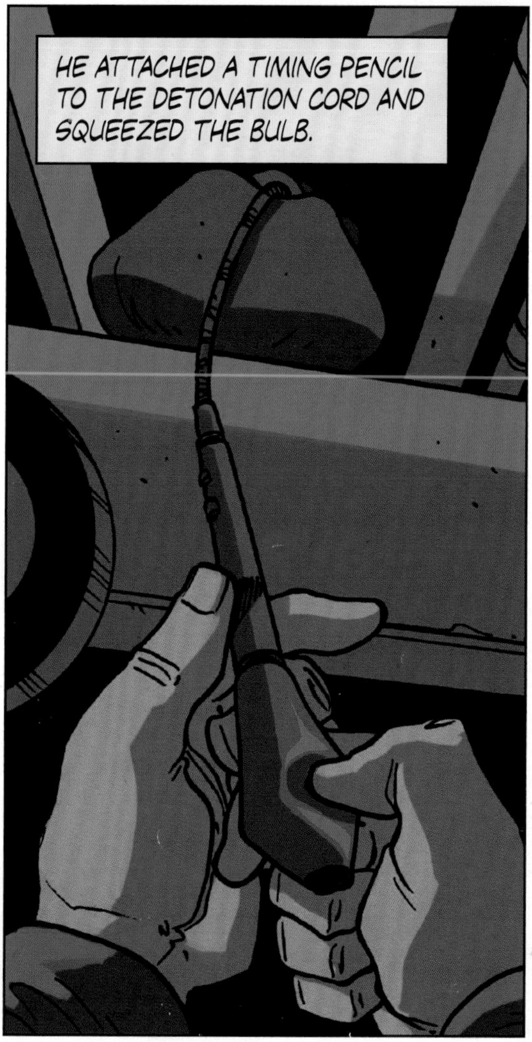
HE ATTACHED A TIMING PENCIL TO THE DETONATION CORD AND SQUEEZED THE BULB.

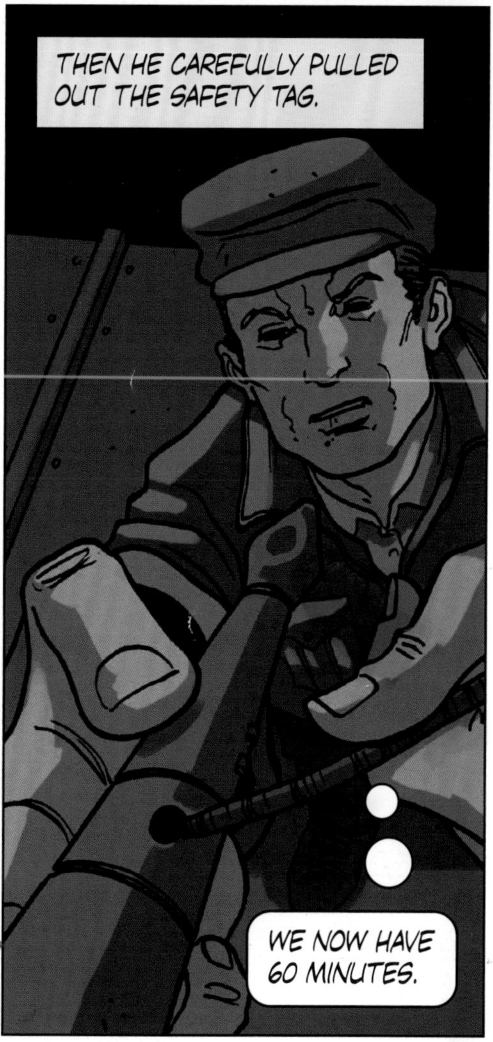
THEN HE CAREFULLY PULLED OUT THE SAFETY TAG.
WE NOW HAVE 60 MINUTES.

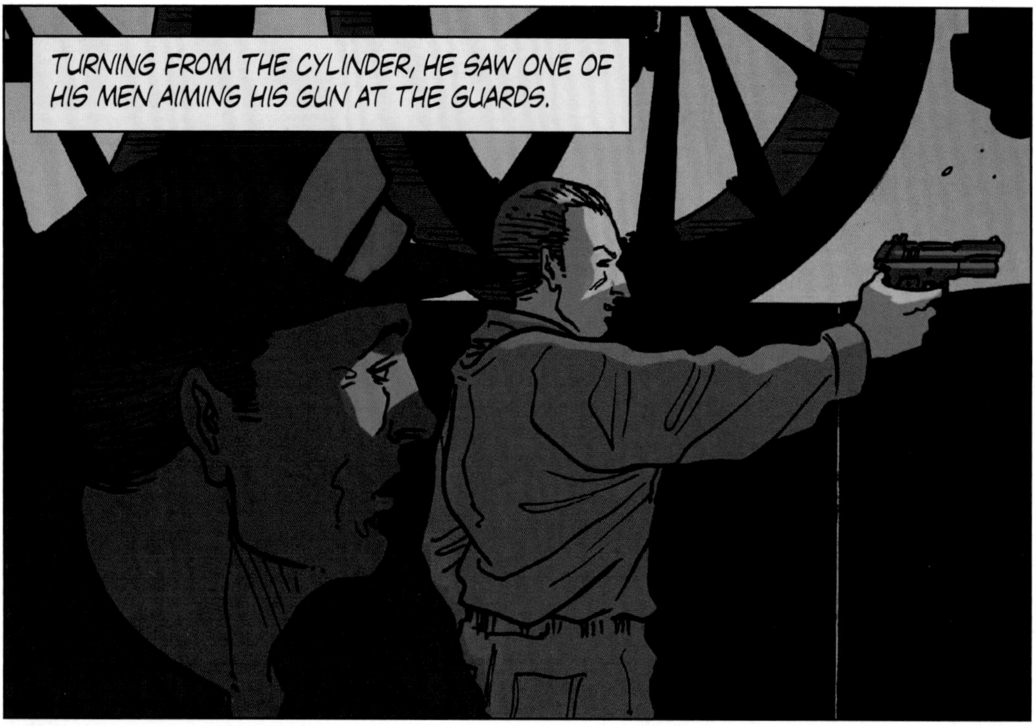
TURNING FROM THE CYLINDER, HE SAW ONE OF HIS MEN AIMING HIS GUN AT THE GUARDS.

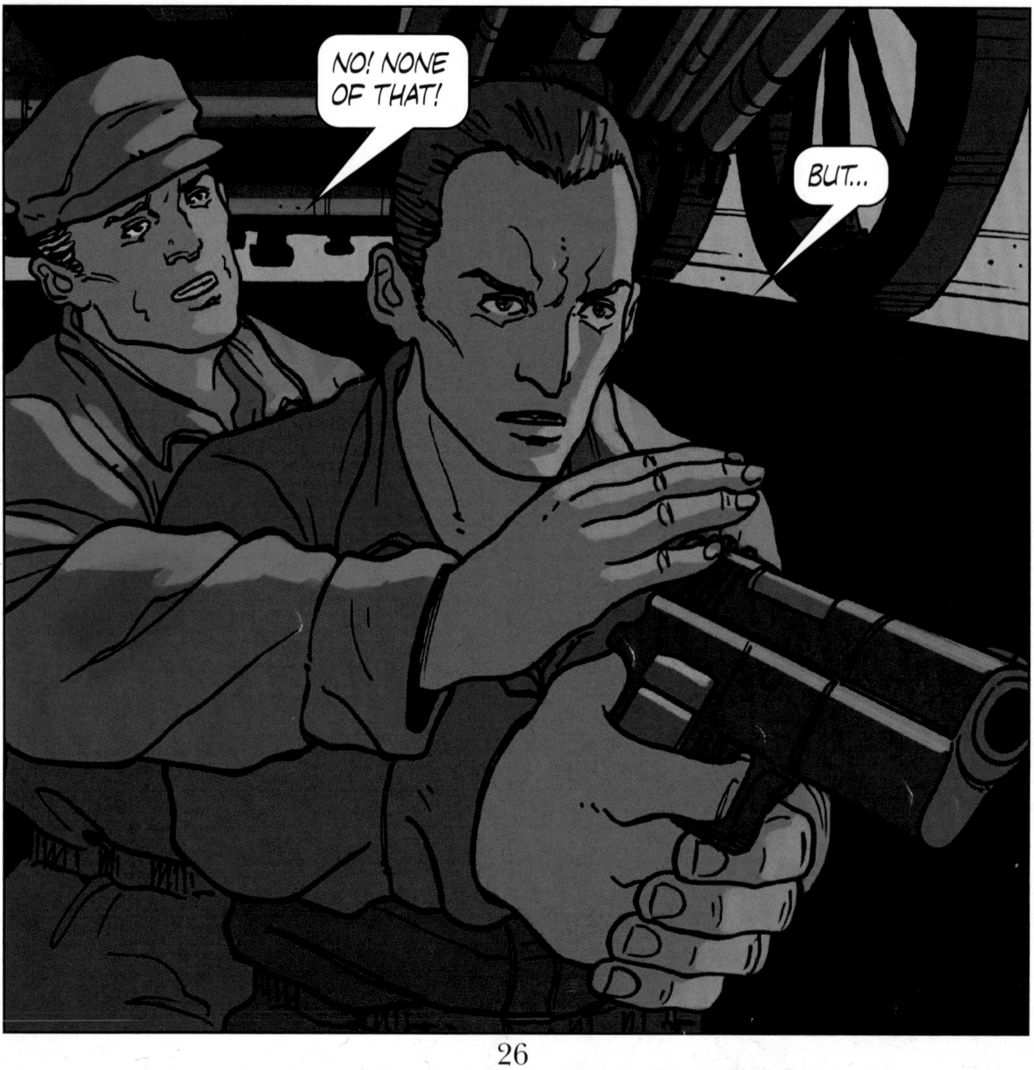
NO! NONE OF THAT!
BUT...

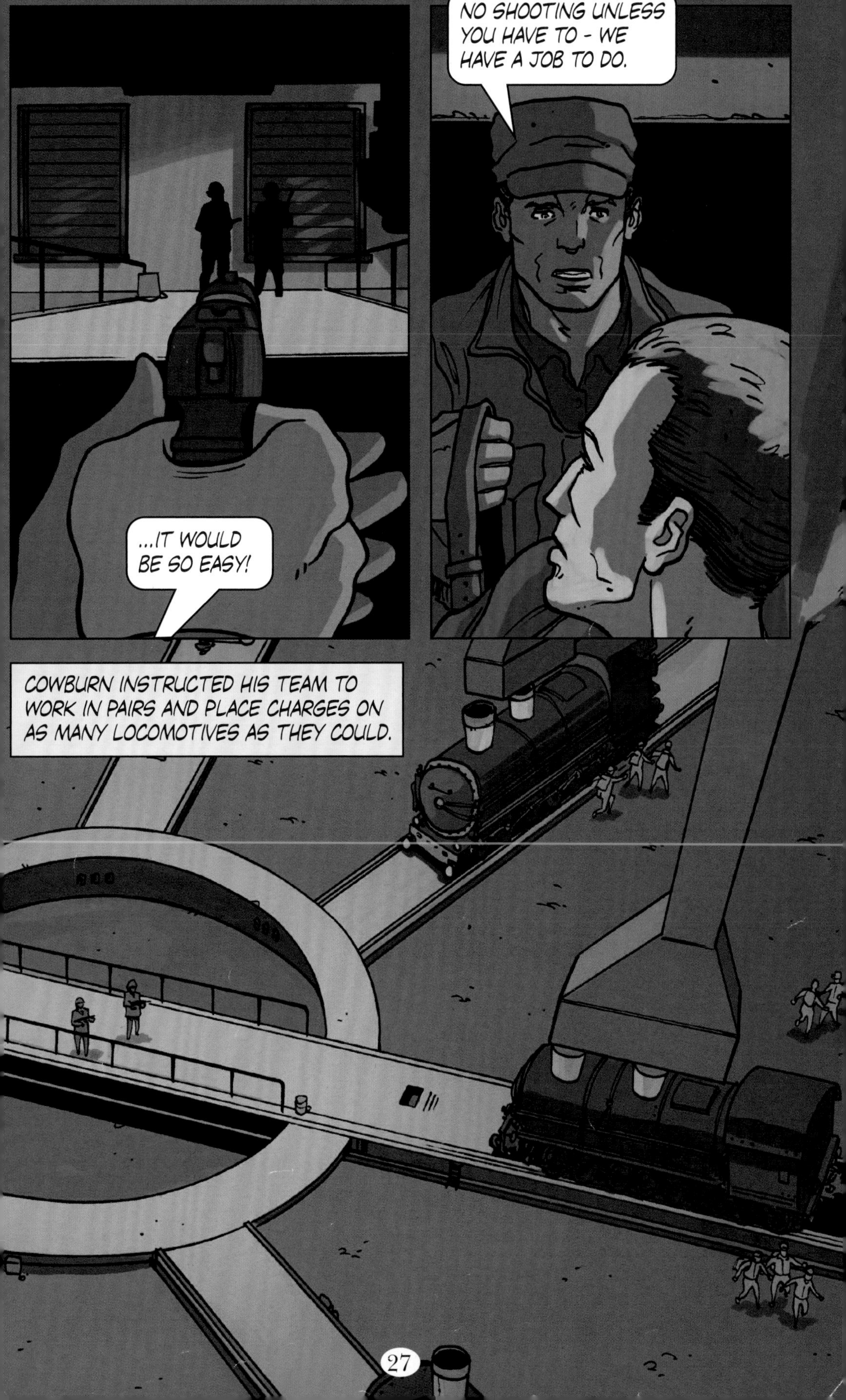
...IT WOULD BE SO EASY!
NO SHOOTING UNLESS YOU HAVE TO - WE HAVE A JOB TO DO.
COWBURN INSTRUCTED HIS TEAM TO WORK IN PAIRS AND PLACE CHARGES ON AS MANY LOCOMOTIVES AS THEY COULD.

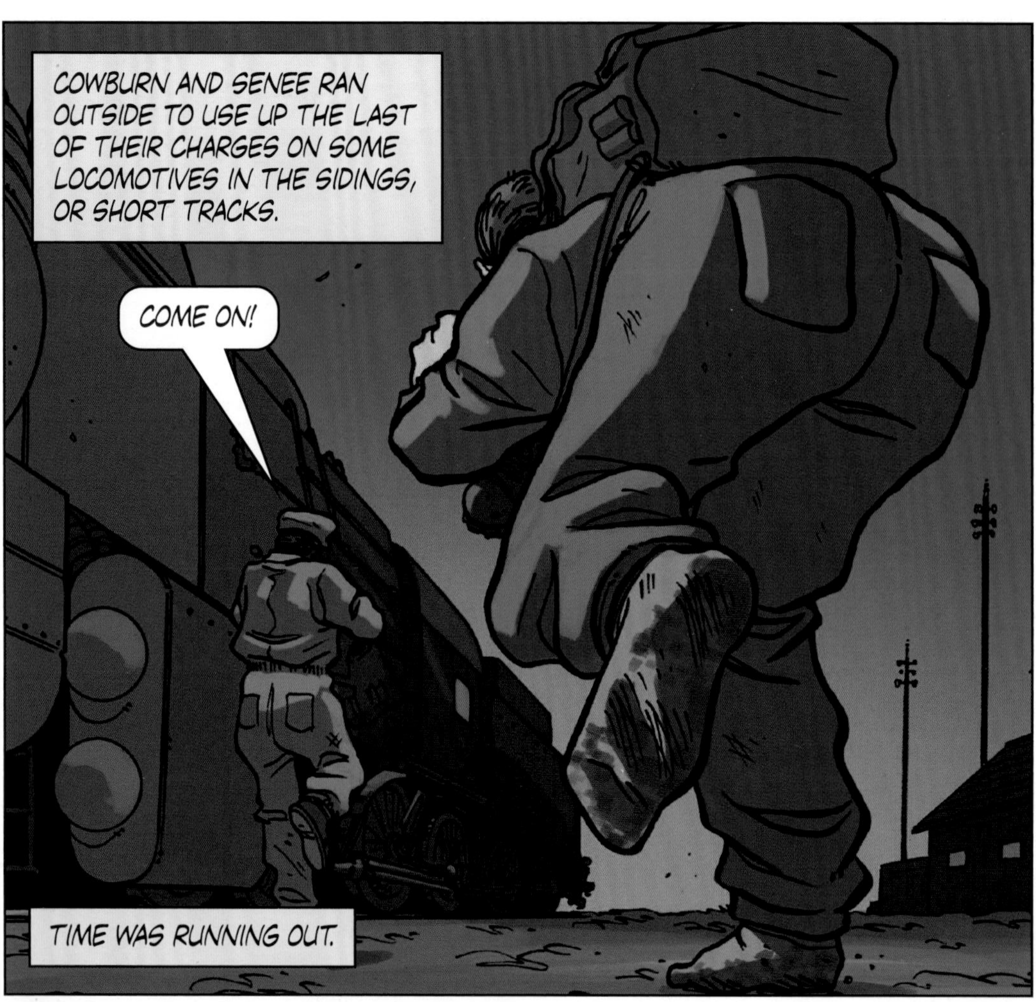
COWBURN AND SENEE RAN OUTSIDE TO USE UP THE LAST OF THEIR CHARGES ON SOME LOCOMOTIVES IN THE SIDINGS, OR SHORT TRACKS.
COME ON!
TIME WAS RUNNING OUT.

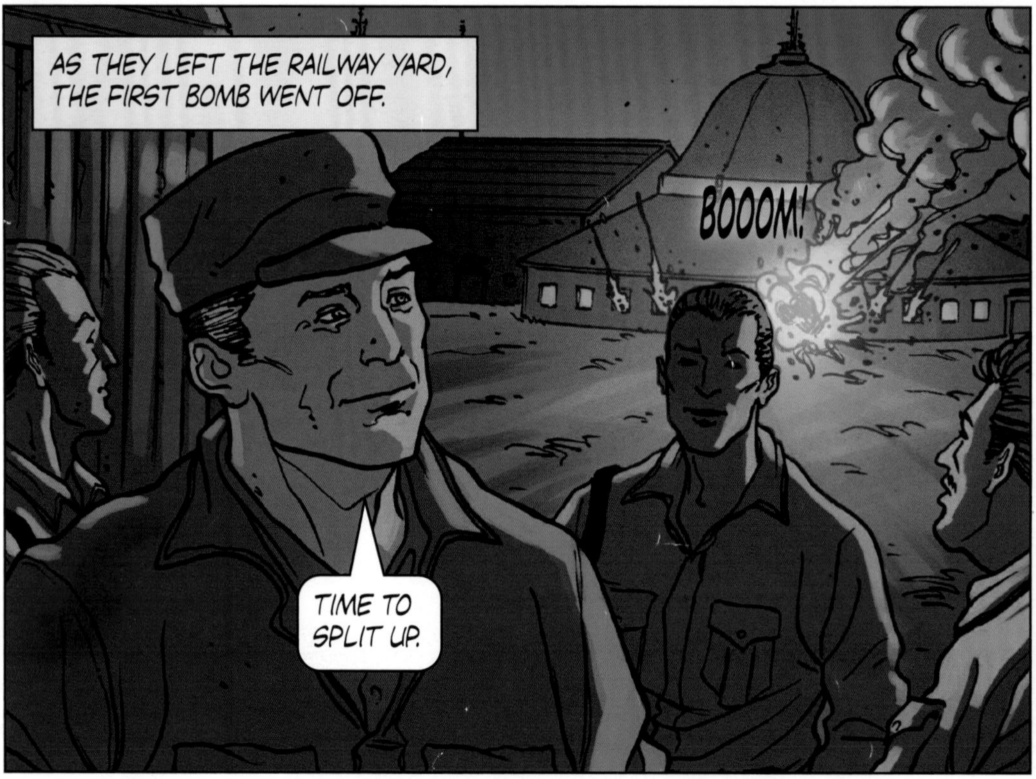
AS THEY LEFT THE RAILWAY YARD, THE FIRST BOMB WENT OFF.
BOOOM!
TIME TO SPLIT UP.

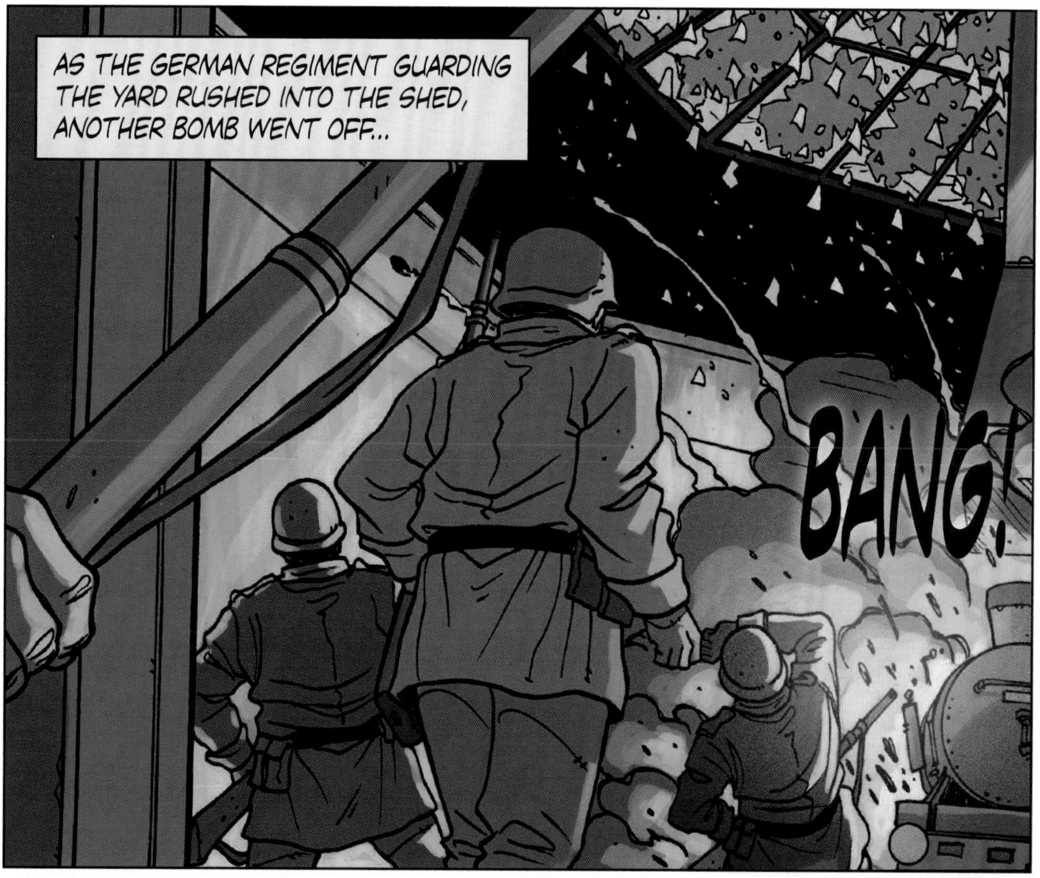
AS THE GERMAN REGIMENT GUARDING THE YARD RUSHED INTO THE SHED, ANOTHER BOMB WENT OFF...
BANG!

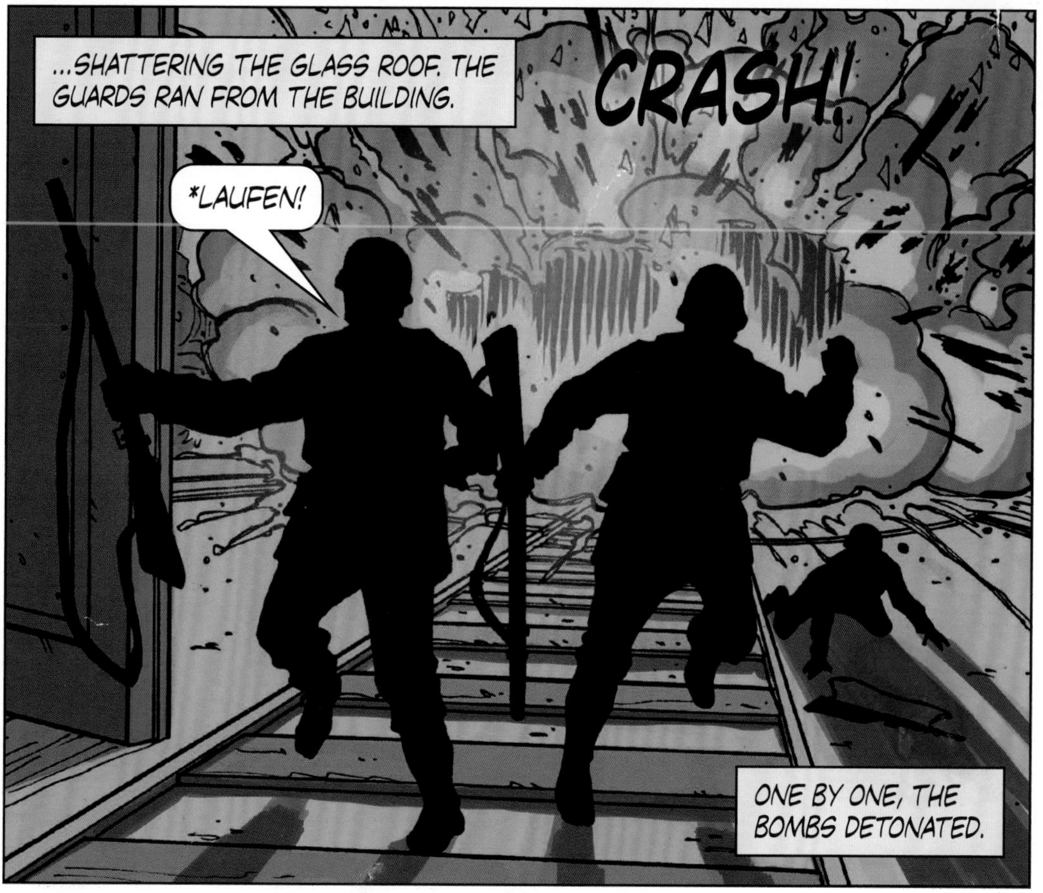
...SHATTERING THE GLASS ROOF. THE GUARDS RAN FROM THE BUILDING.
CRASH!
*LAUFEN!
ONE BY ONE, THE BOMBS DETONATED.

*RUN!

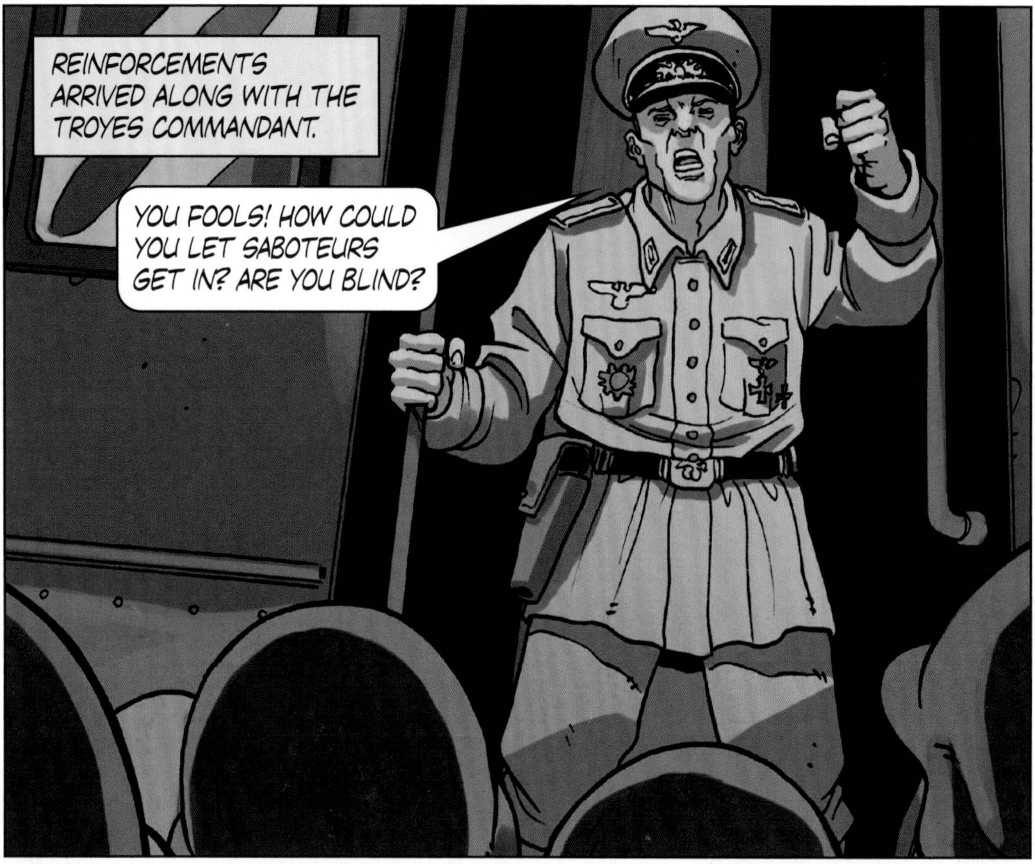
REINFORCEMENTS ARRIVED ALONG WITH THE TROYES COMMANDANT.
YOU FOOLS! HOW COULD YOU LET SABOTEURS GET IN? ARE YOU BLIND?

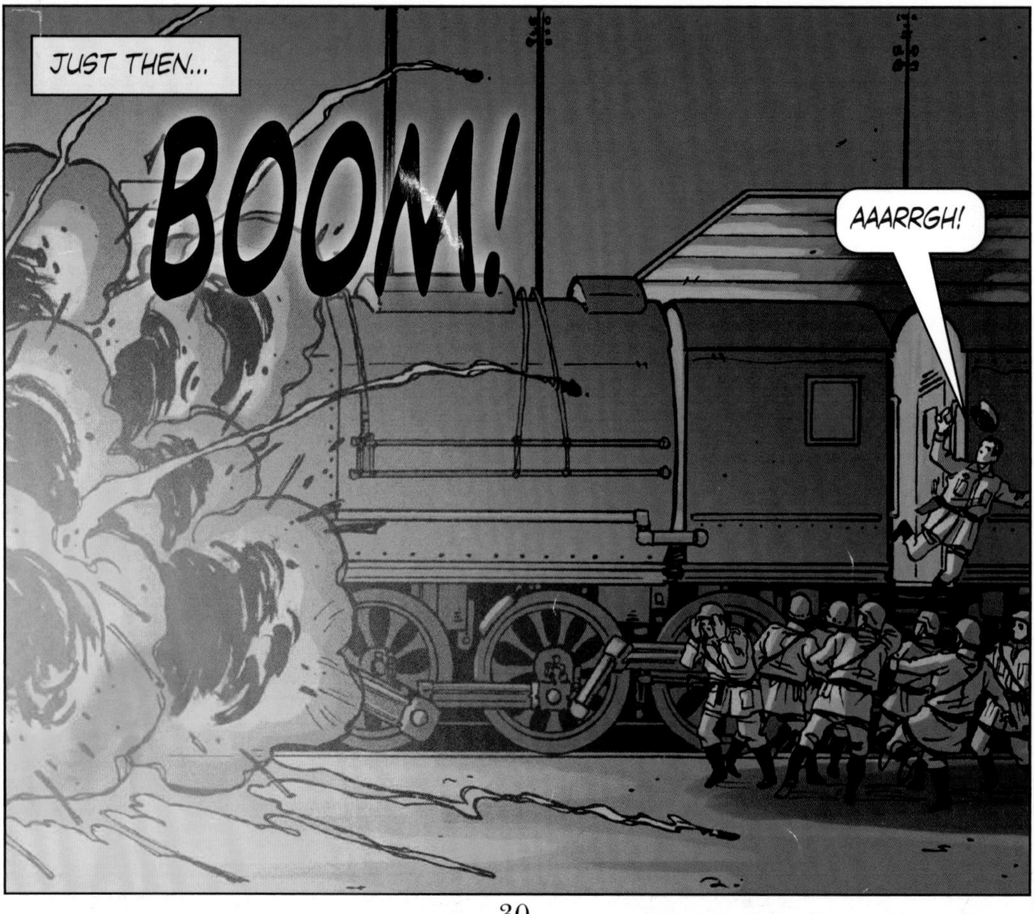
JUST THEN...
BOOM!
AAARRGH!

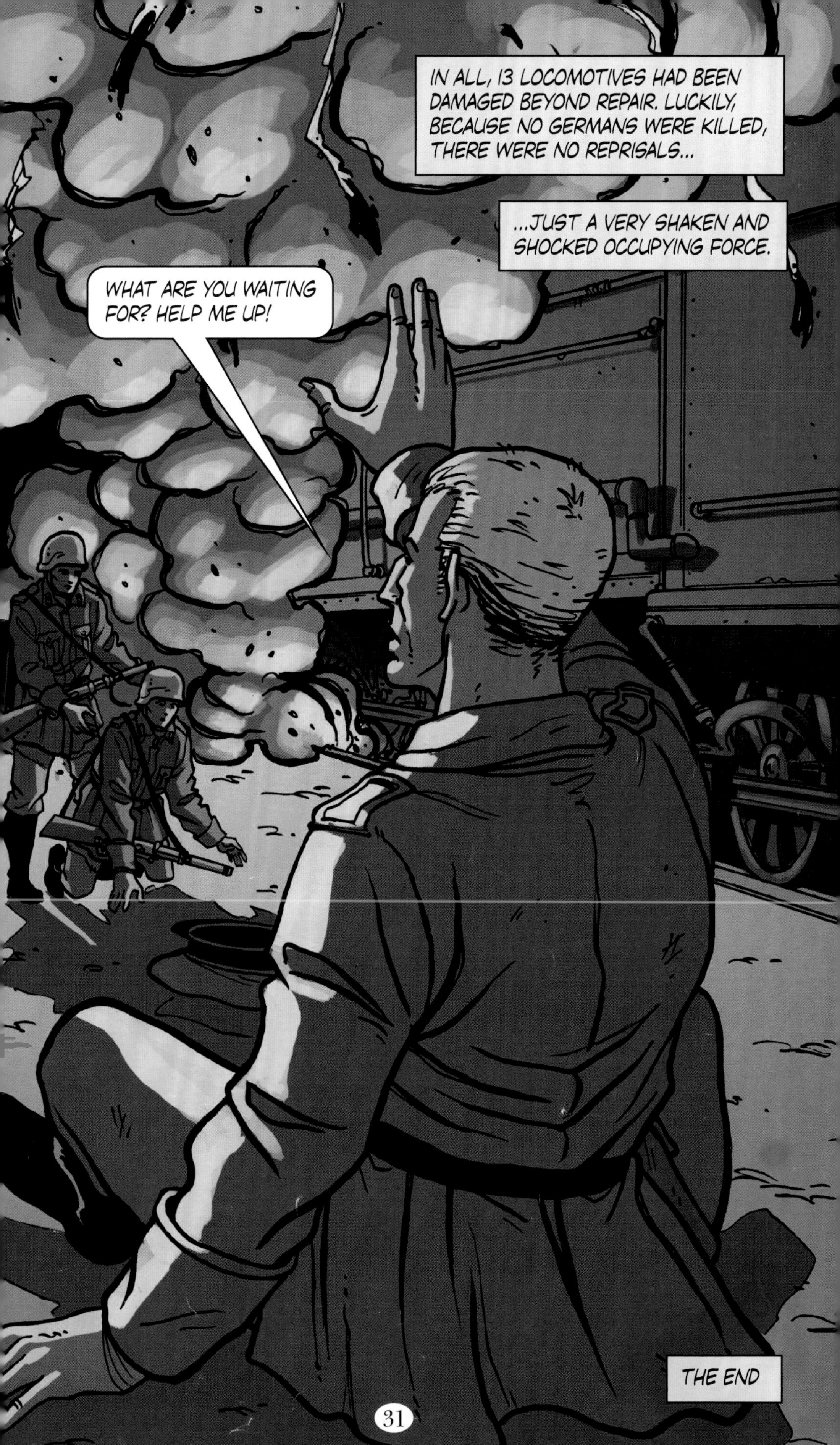
IN ALL, 13 LOCOMOTIVES HAD BEEN DAMAGED BEYOND REPAIR. LUCKILY, BECAUSE NO GERMANS WERE KILLED, THERE WERE NO REPRISALS...
...JUST A VERY SHAKEN AND SHOCKED OCCUPYING FORCE.
WHAT ARE YOU WAITING FOR? HELP ME UP!
THE END

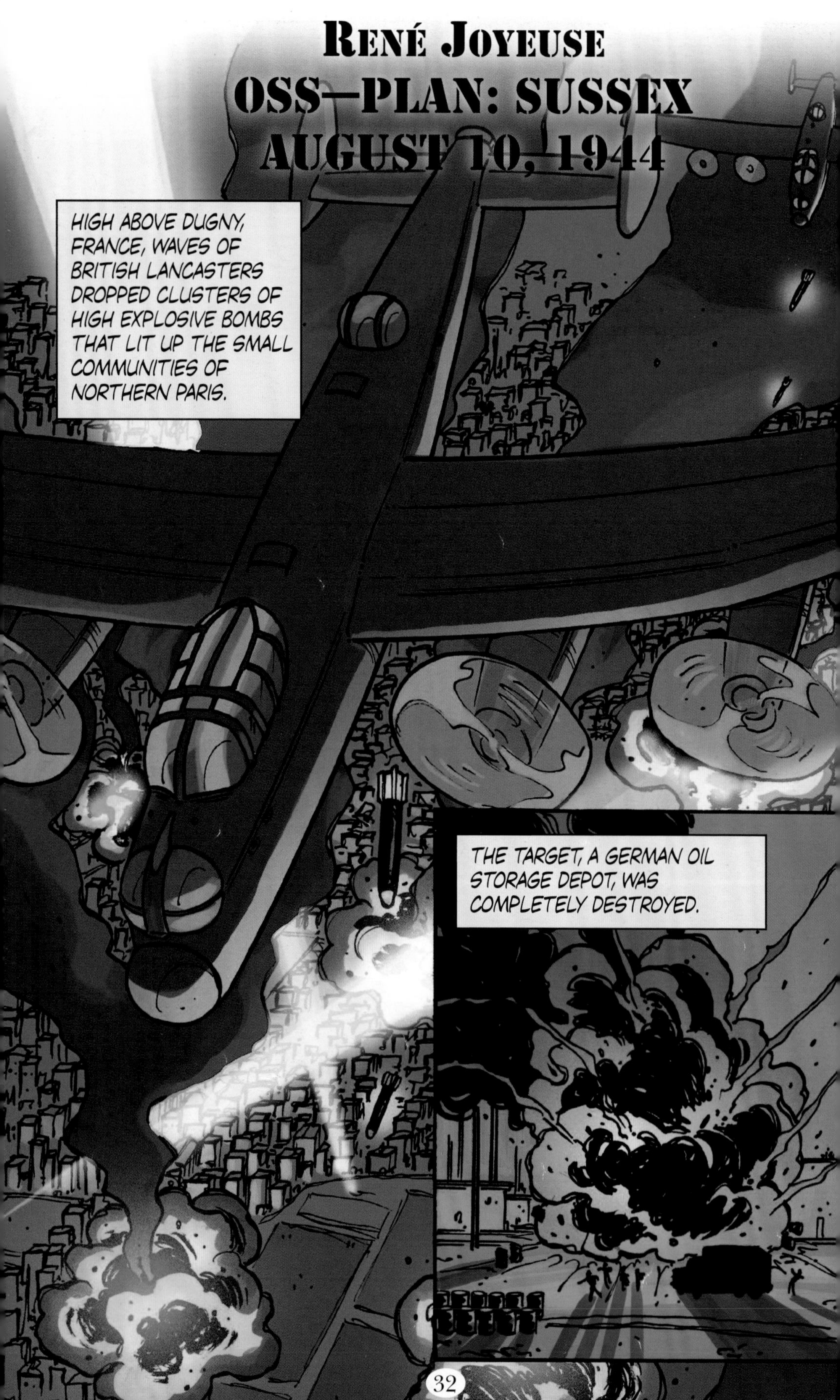
RENÉ JOYEUSE
OSS—PLAN: SUSSEX
AUGUST 10, 1944
HIGH ABOVE DUGNY, FRANCE, WAVES OF BRITISH LANCASTERS DROPPED CLUSTERS OF HIGH EXPLOSIVE BOMBS THAT LIT UP THE SMALL COMMUNITIES OF NORTHERN PARIS.
THE TARGET, A GERMAN OIL STORAGE DEPOT, WAS COMPLETELY DESTROYED.

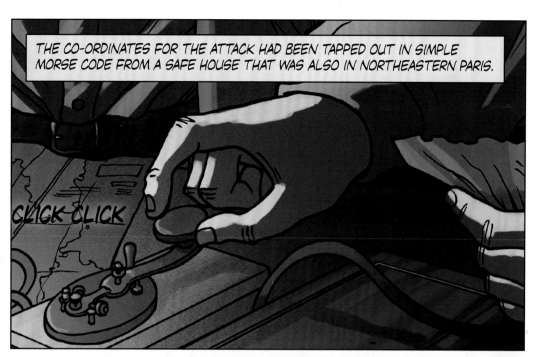

THE CO-ORDINATES FOR THE ATTACK HAD BEEN TAPPED OUT IN SIMPLE MORSE CODE FROM A SAFE HOUSE THAT WAS ALSO IN NORTHEASTERN PARIS.

CLICK CLICK

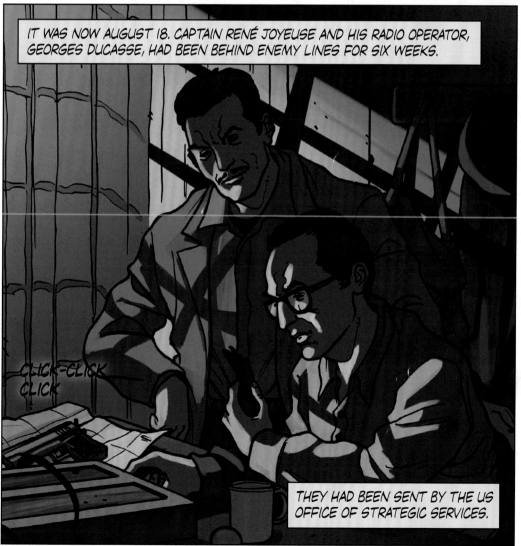

IT WAS NOW AUGUST 18. CAPTAIN RENÉ JOYEUSE AND HIS RADIO OPERATOR, GEORGES DUCASSE, HAD BEEN BEHIND ENEMY LINES FOR SIX WEEKS.

CLICK-CLICK CLICK

THEY HAD BEEN SENT BY THE US OFFICE OF STRATEGIC SERVICES.

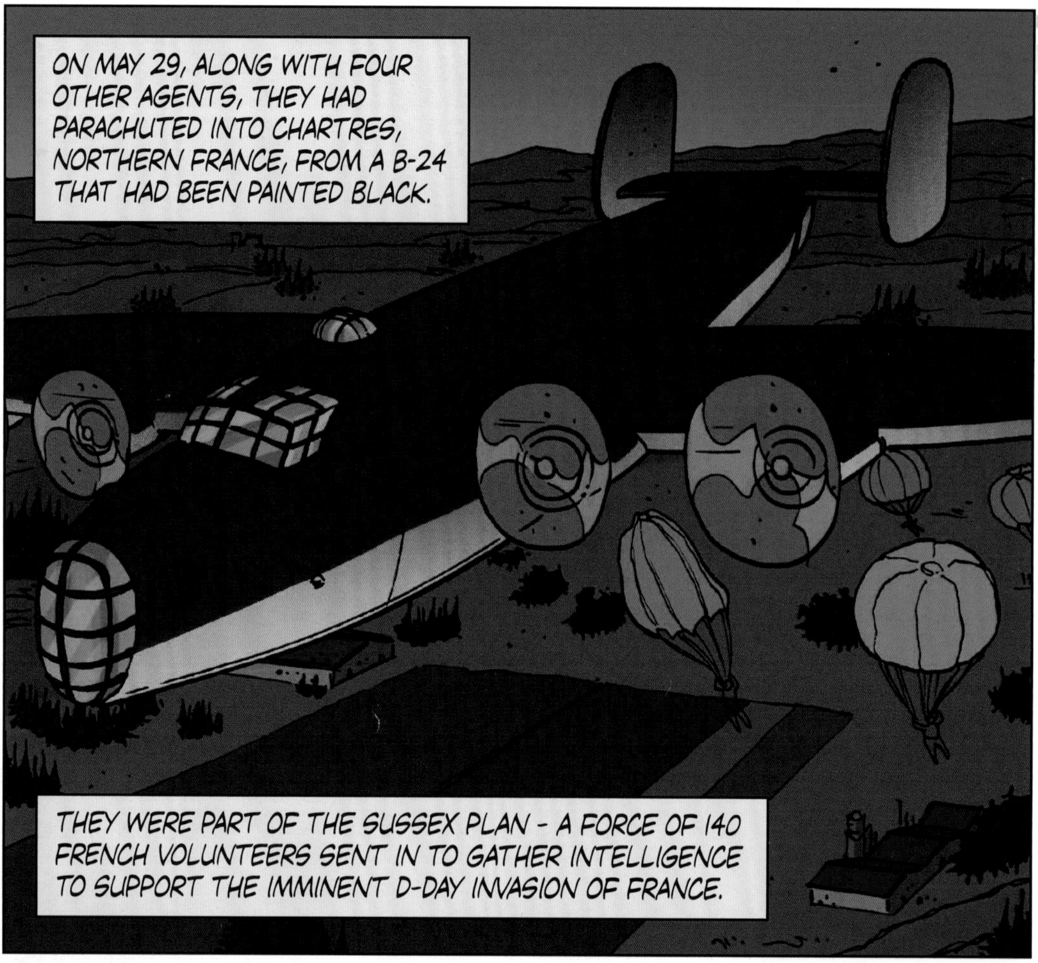
ON MAY 29, ALONG WITH FOUR OTHER AGENTS, THEY HAD PARACHUTED INTO CHARTRES, NORTHERN FRANCE, FROM A B-24 THAT HAD BEEN PAINTED BLACK.
THEY WERE PART OF THE SUSSEX PLAN - A FORCE OF 140 FRENCH VOLUNTEERS SENT IN TO GATHER INTELLIGENCE TO SUPPORT THE IMMINENT D-DAY INVASION OF FRANCE.

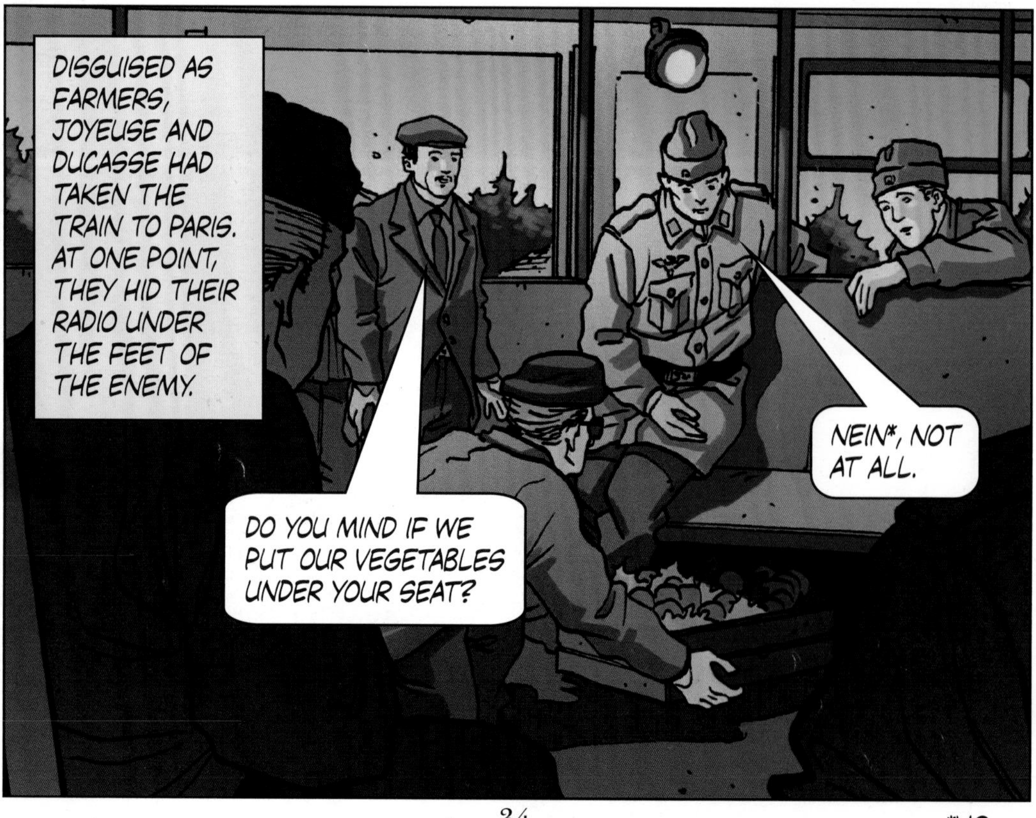
DISGUISED AS FARMERS, JOYEUSE AND DUCASSE HAD TAKEN THE TRAIN TO PARIS. AT ONE POINT, THEY HID THEIR RADIO UNDER THE FEET OF THE ENEMY.
DO YOU MIND IF WE PUT OUR VEGETABLES UNDER YOUR SEAT?
NEIN*, NOT AT ALL.

*NO

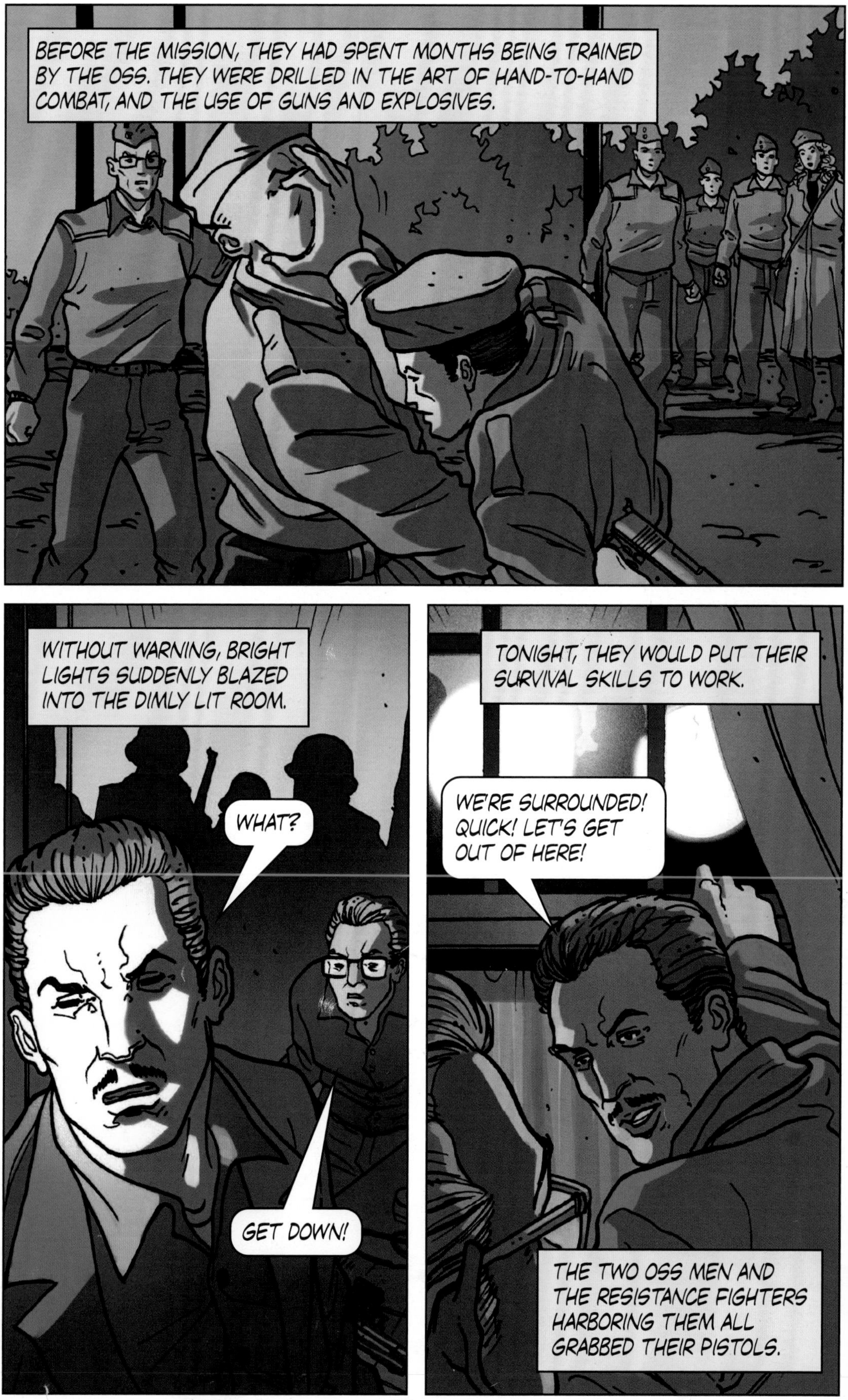
BEFORE THE MISSION, THEY HAD SPENT MONTHS BEING TRAINED BY THE OSS. THEY WERE DRILLED IN THE ART OF HAND-TO-HAND COMBAT, AND THE USE OF GUNS AND EXPLOSIVES.
WITHOUT WARNING, BRIGHT LIGHTS SUDDENLY BLAZED INTO THE DIMLY LIT ROOM.
WHAT?
GET DOWN!
TONIGHT, THEY WOULD PUT THEIR SURVIVAL SKILLS TO WORK.
WE'RE SURROUNDED! QUICK! LET'S GET OUT OF HERE!
THE TWO OSS MEN AND THE RESISTANCE FIGHTERS HARBORING THEM ALL GRABBED THEIR PISTOLS.

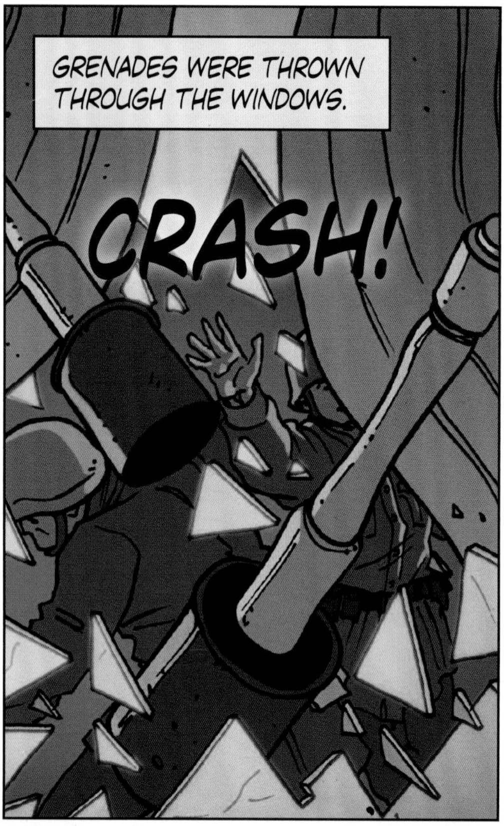
GRENADES WERE THROWN THROUGH THE WINDOWS.
CRASH!

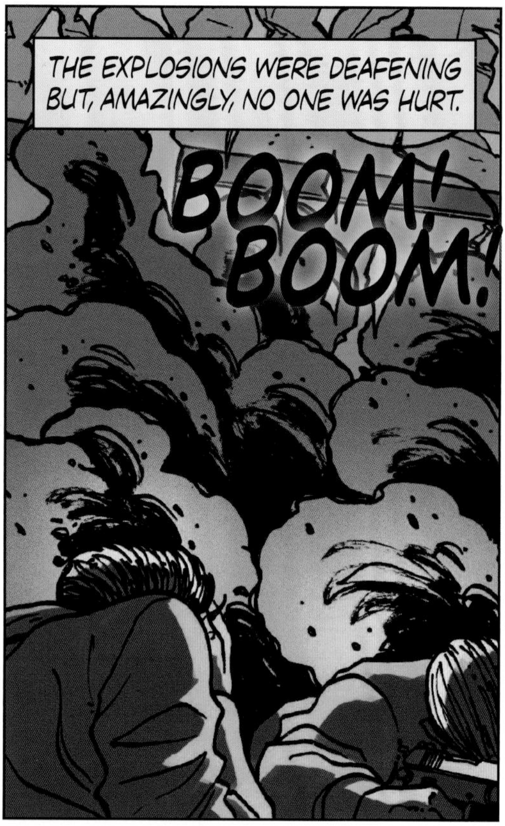
THE EXPLOSIONS WERE DEAFENING BUT, AMAZINGLY, NO ONE WAS HURT.
BOOM!
BOOM!

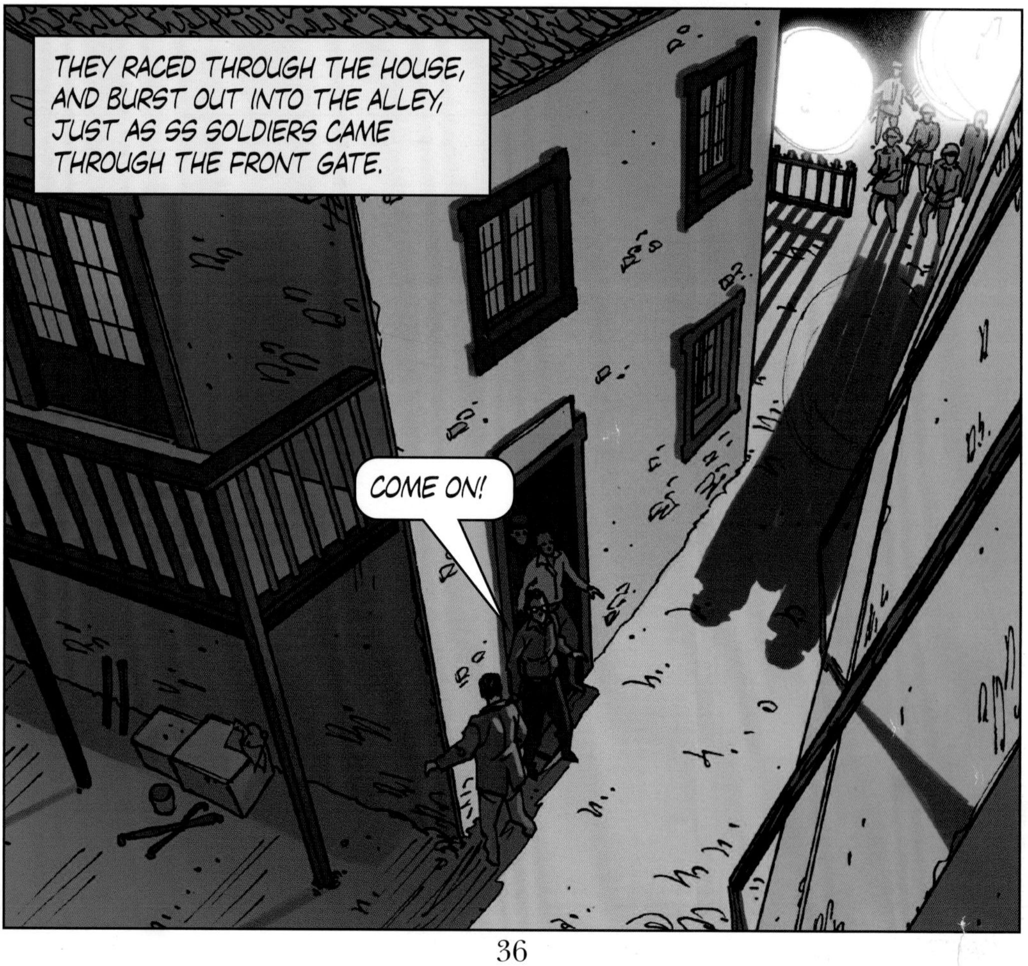
THEY RACED THROUGH THE HOUSE, AND BURST OUT INTO THE ALLEY, JUST AS SS SOLDIERS CAME THROUGH THE FRONT GATE.
COME ON!

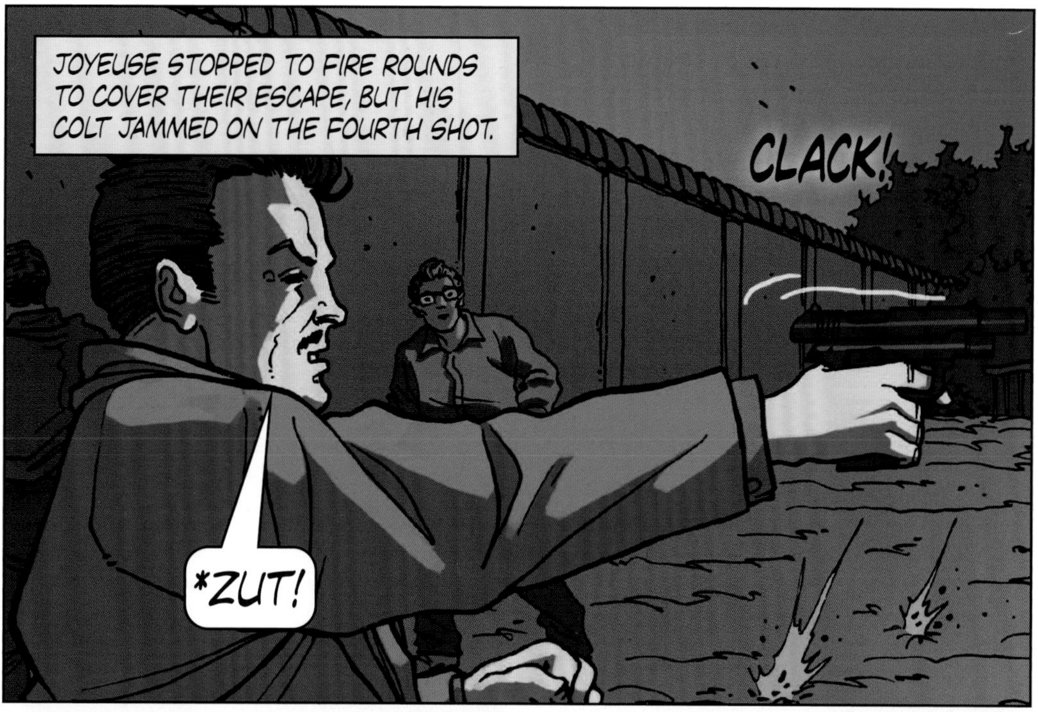
JOYEUSE STOPPED TO FIRE ROUNDS TO COVER THEIR ESCAPE, BUT HIS COLT JAMMED ON THE FOURTH SHOT.
CLACK!
*ZUT!

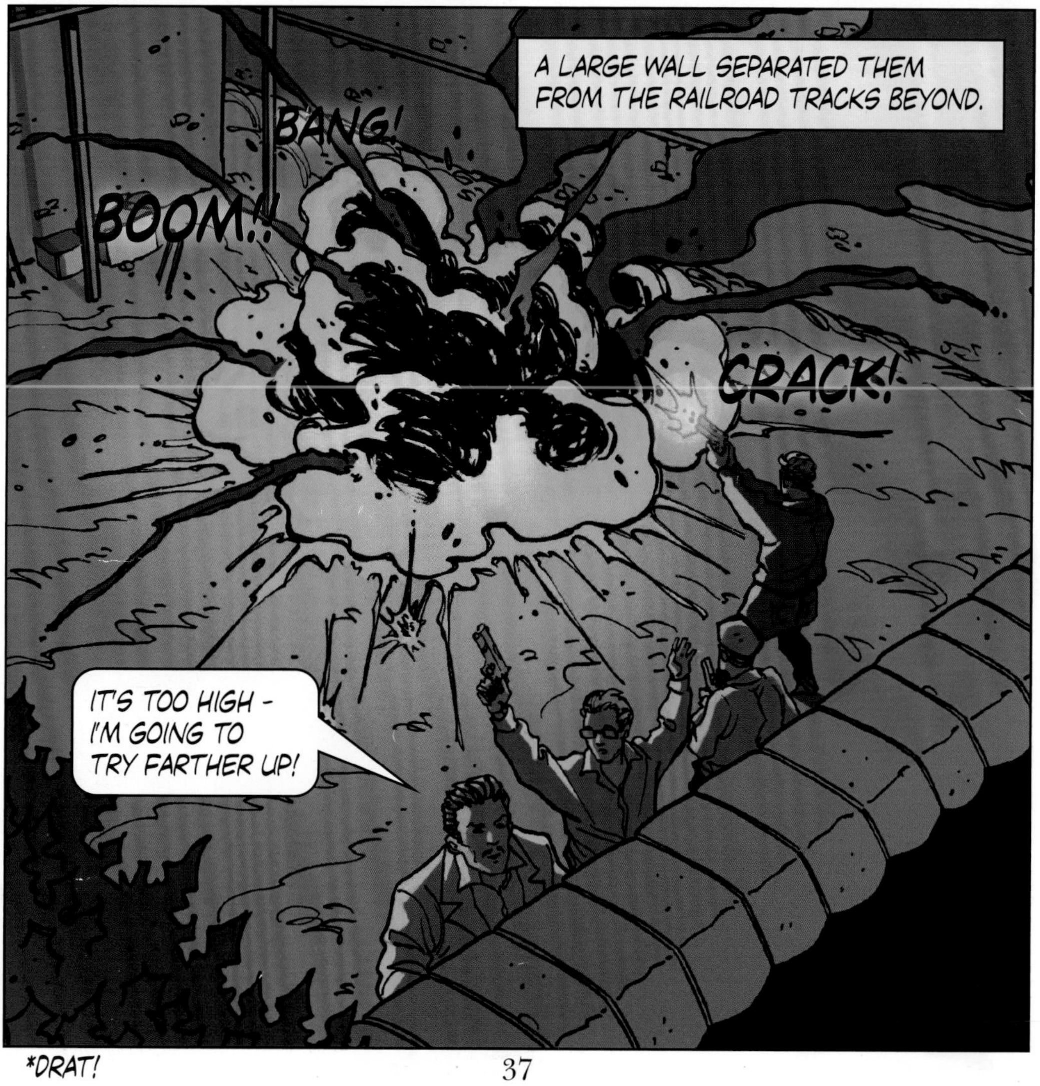
A LARGE WALL SEPARATED THEM FROM THE RAILROAD TRACKS BEYOND.
BANG!
BOOM!!
CRACK!
IT'S TOO HIGH - I'M GOING TO TRY FARTHER UP!

*DRAT!

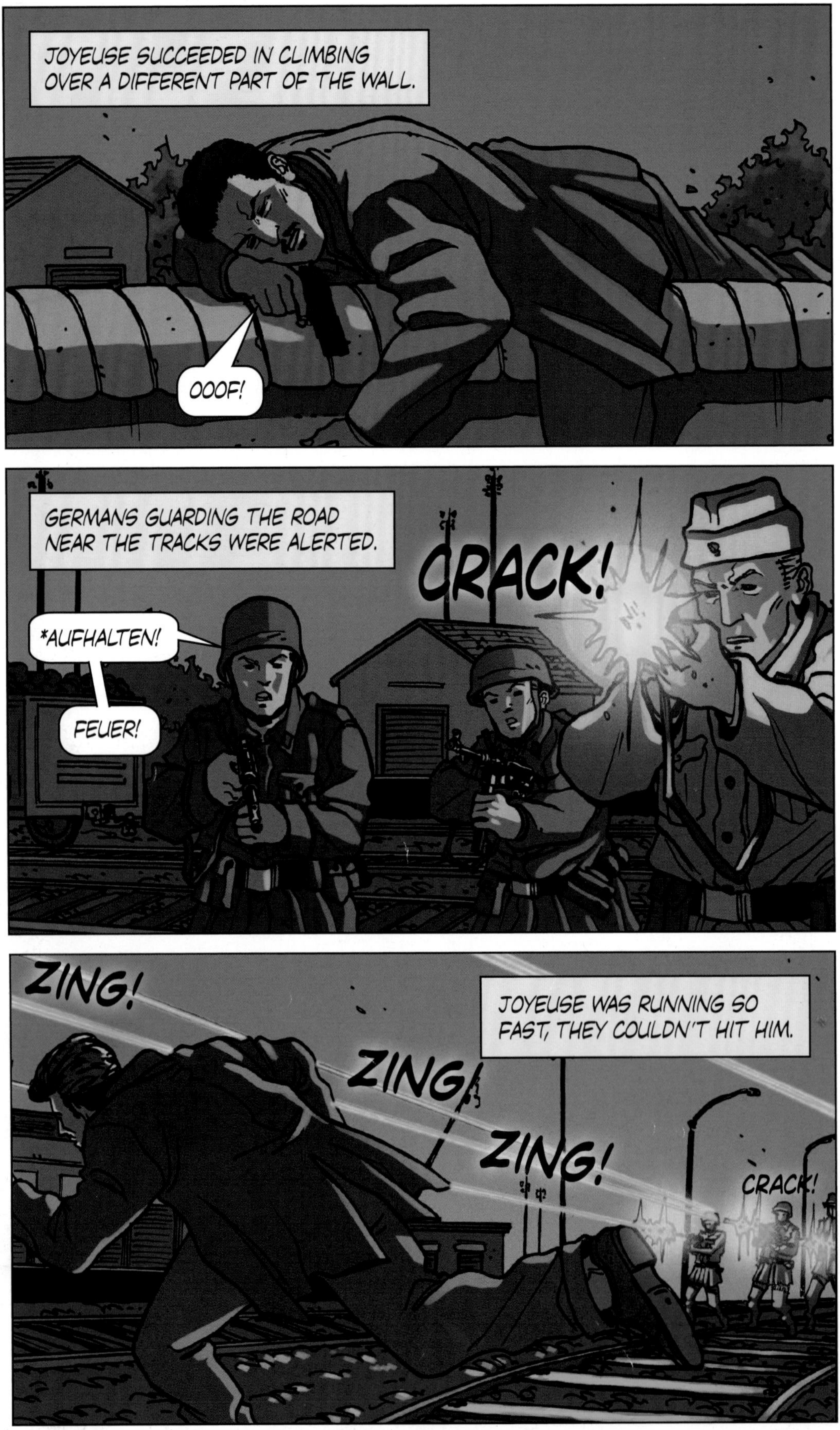
JOYEUSE SUCCEEDED IN CLIMBING OVER A DIFFERENT PART OF THE WALL.
OOOF!
GERMANS GUARDING THE ROAD NEAR THE TRACKS WERE ALERTED.
CRACK!
*AUFHALTEN!
FEUER!
ZING!
JOYEUSE WAS RUNNING SO FAST, THEY COULDN'T HIT HIM.
ZING!
ZING!
CRACK!

*STOP THEM! FIRE!

HE CROSSED THE TRACKS WITH THE GERMANS IN HOT PURSUIT.

*IHN STOPPEN!

HE QUICKLY CLIMBED OVER A GATE, THEN CROUCHED DOWN BEHIND A LOW WALL AS THE GERMANS EMPTIED THEIR MAGAZINES IN HIS DIRECTION.

DRRRRRRRRRRRRRRRRRRRRRR

PEOW!

PANG!

*STOP HIM!

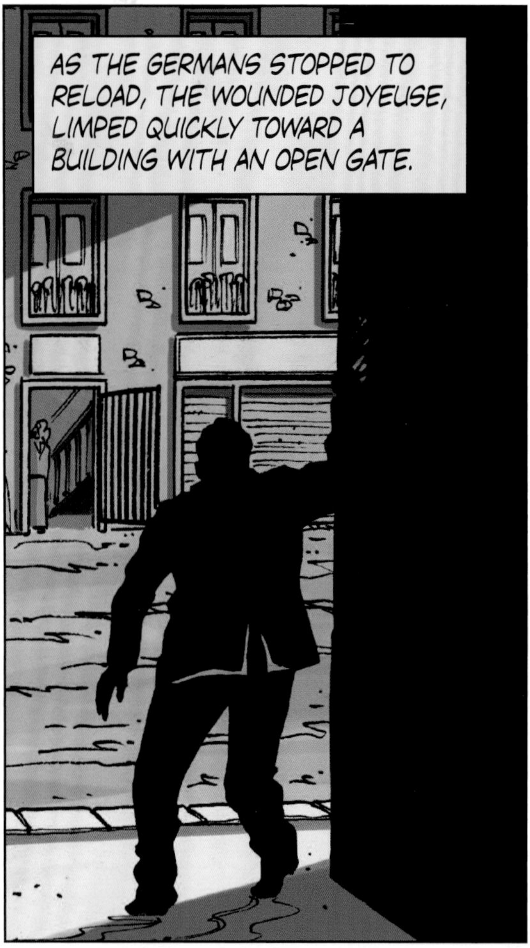
AS THE GERMANS STOPPED TO RELOAD, THE WOUNDED JOYEUSE, LIMPED QUICKLY TOWARD A BUILDING WITH AN OPEN GATE.

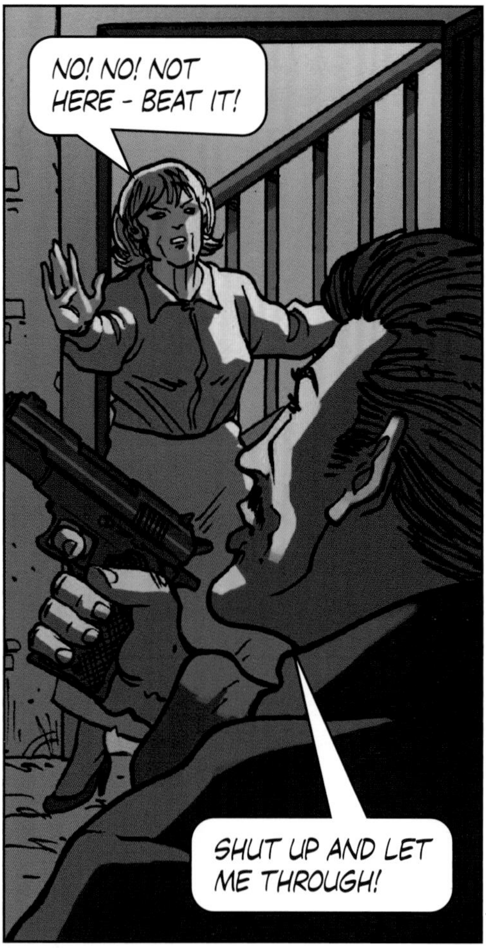
NO! NO! NOT HERE - BEAT IT!
SHUT UP AND LET ME THROUGH!

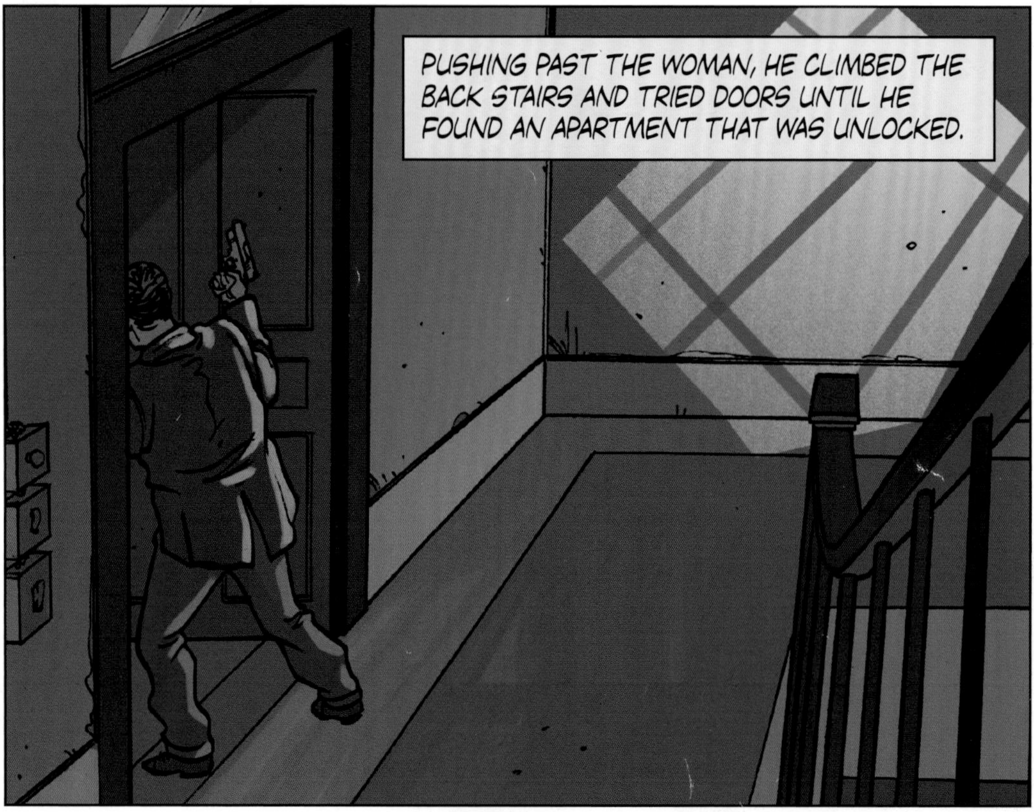
PUSHING PAST THE WOMAN, HE CLIMBED THE BACK STAIRS AND TRIED DOORS UNTIL HE FOUND AN APARTMENT THAT WAS UNLOCKED.

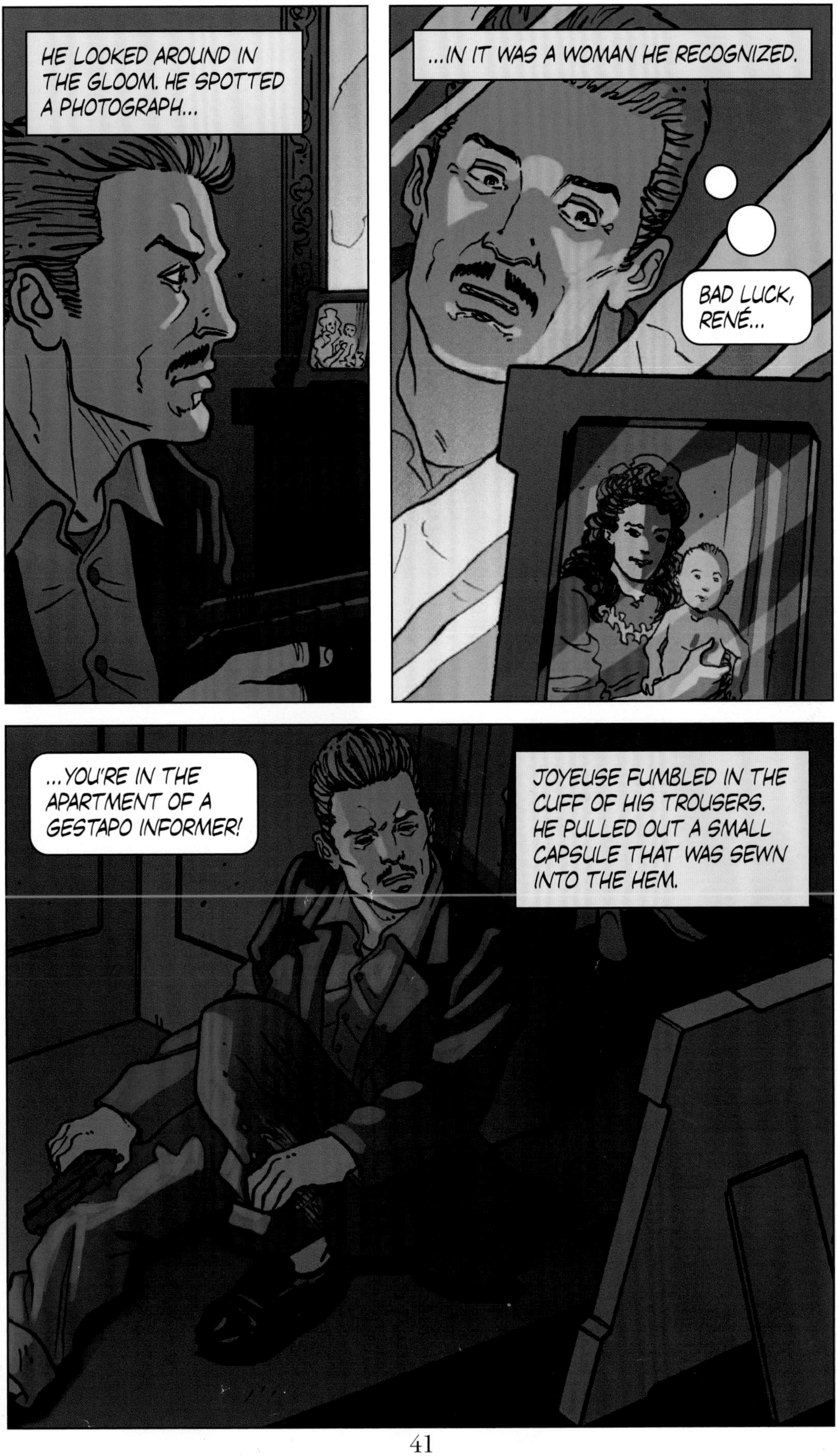
HE LOOKED AROUND IN THE GLOOM. HE SPOTTED A PHOTOGRAPH...
...IN IT WAS A WOMAN HE RECOGNIZED.
BAD LUCK, RENÉ...
...YOU'RE IN THE APARTMENT OF A GESTAPO INFORMER!
JOYEUSE FUMBLED IN THE CUFF OF HIS TROUSERS. HE PULLED OUT A SMALL CAPSULE THAT WAS SEWN INTO THE HEM.

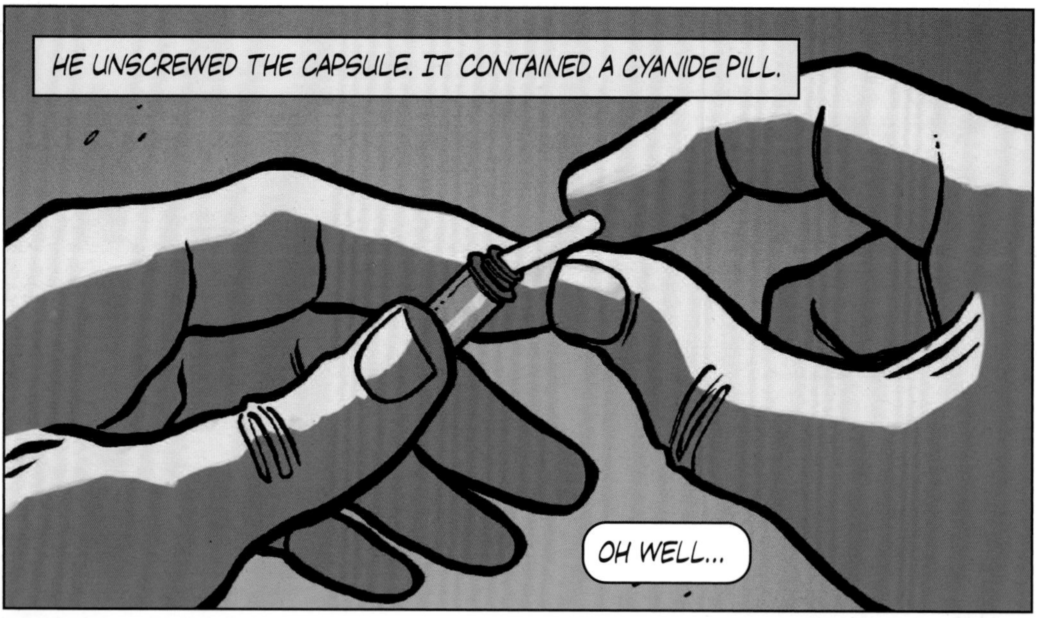
HE UNSCREWED THE CAPSULE. IT CONTAINED A CYANIDE PILL.
OH WELL...

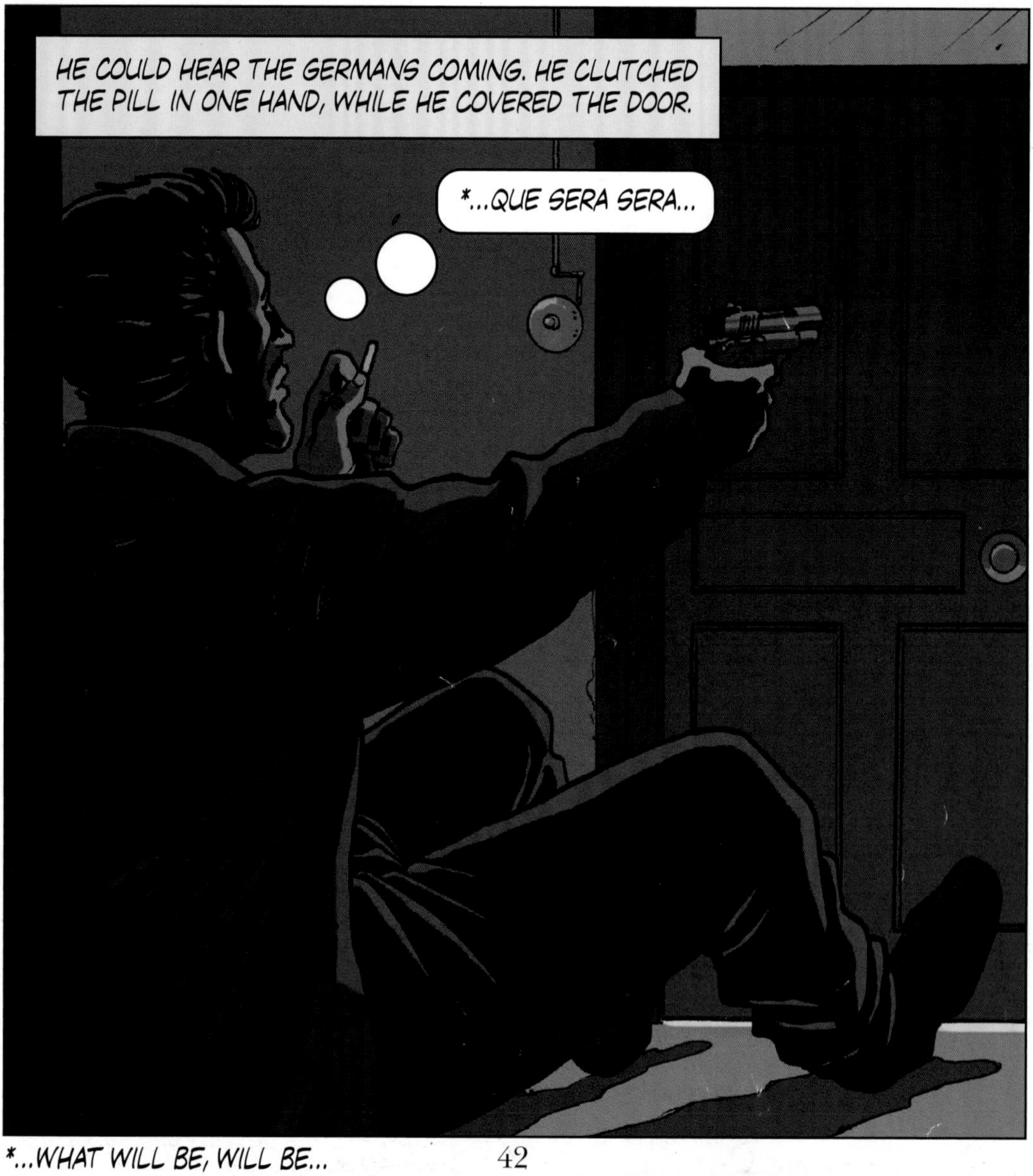
HE COULD HEAR THE GERMANS COMING. HE CLUTCHED THE PILL IN ONE HAND, WHILE HE COVERED THE DOOR.
*...QUE SERA SERA...

*...WHAT WILL BE, WILL BE...

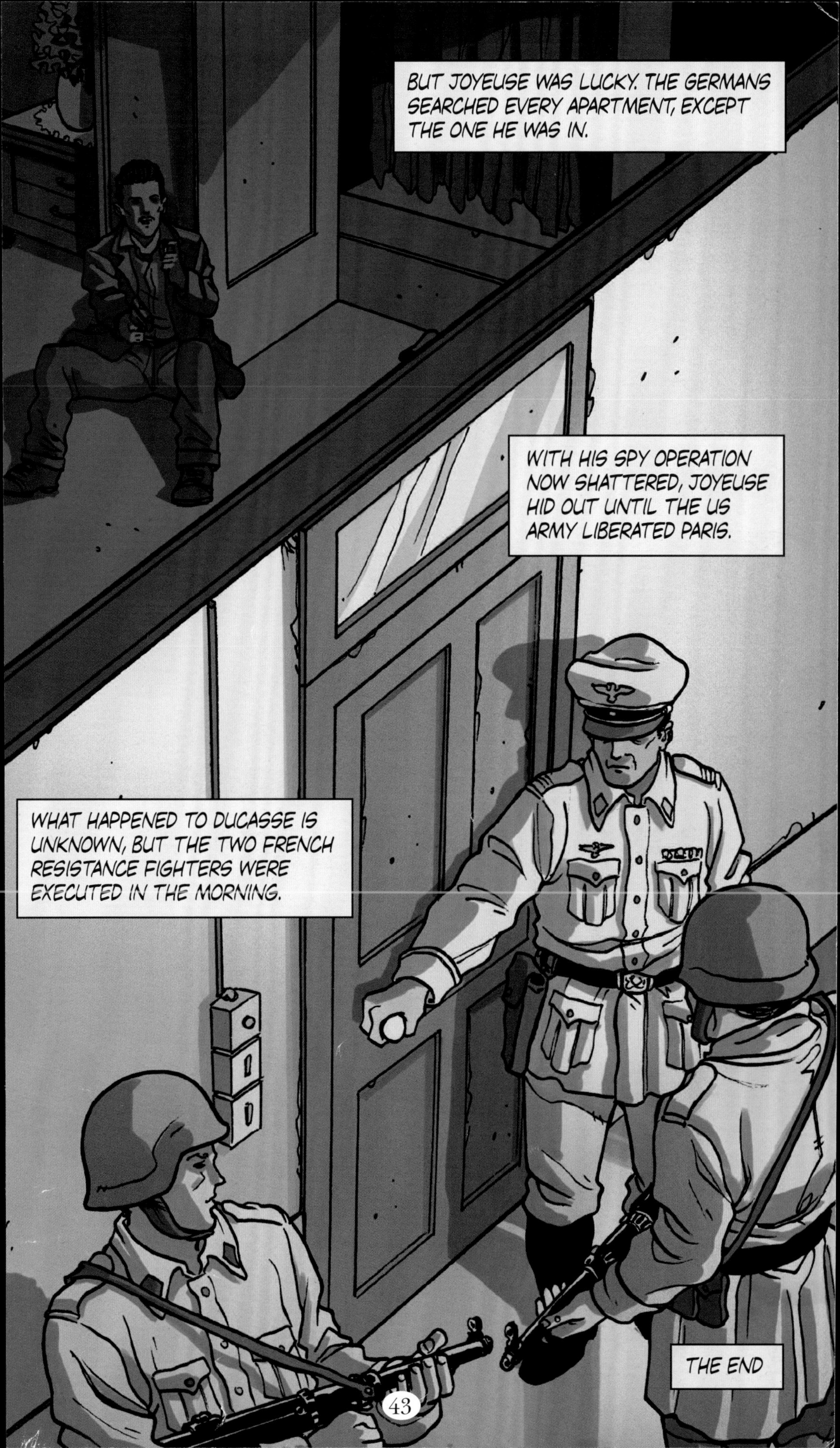
BUT JOYEUSE WAS LUCKY. THE GERMANS SEARCHED EVERY APARTMENT, EXCEPT THE ONE HE WAS IN.
WITH HIS SPY OPERATION NOW SHATTERED, JOYEUSE HID OUT UNTIL THE US ARMY LIBERATED PARIS.
WHAT HAPPENED TO DUCASSE IS UNKNOWN, BUT THE TWO FRENCH RESISTANCE FIGHTERS WERE EXECUTED IN THE MORNING.
THE END

SECRET WEAPONS

On February 28, 1943, six SOE-trained Norwegian commandos executed a daring raid that crippled the heavy water plant at Vemork in occupied Norway. Further Allied bombing put the plant out of action permanently. The atomic bomb was a secret weapon the Germans would never have.

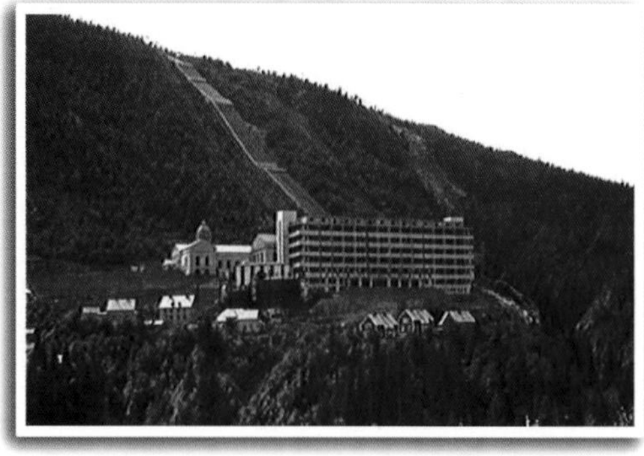

Even though it lacked scientists and money, the Vemork plant was crucial to Germany's nuclear weapons ambitions.

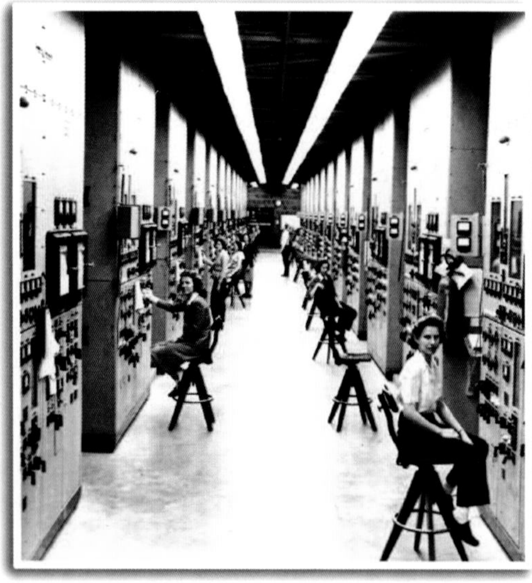

Workers at industrial plants making nuclear material were kept in the dark about what they were producing. Enemy sabotage acts, like those committed in the United States during World War 1 (below), were an ever-present danger.

The Manhattan Project

While Germany's atomic research program was being disabled, in the United States an enormous military/industrial effort was underway to complete the world's first-ever nuclear weapon.

The top secret Manhattan Project began in 1942 and involved huge numbers of military and civilian personnel, including many scientists who had fled Nazi oppression. The project overseer, General Leslie R. Groves, conceived a security operation so tight that the atom bomb was the best-kept secret of the war.

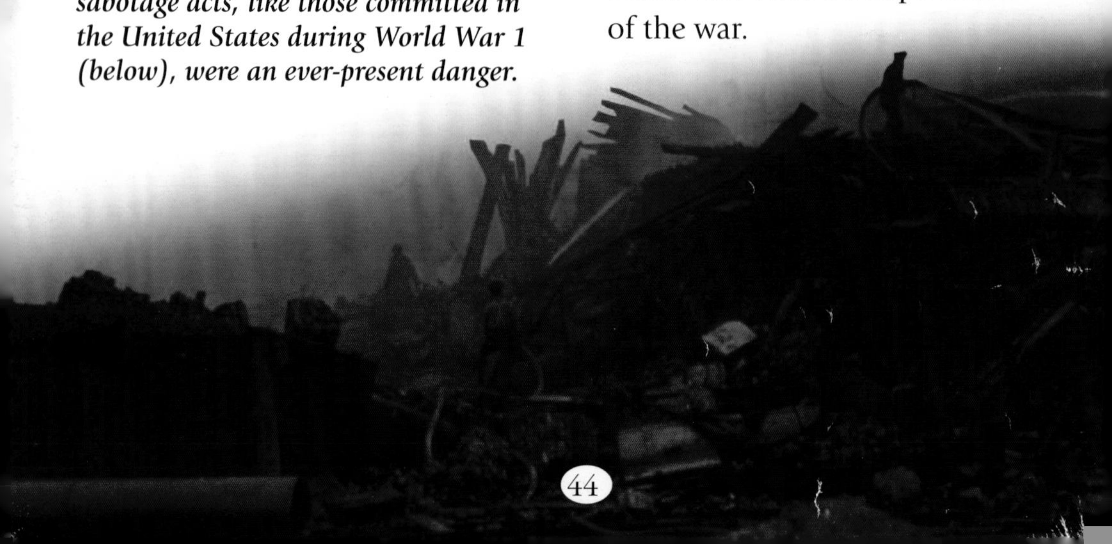

VENGEANCE WEAPONS

On June 6, 1944, the Allies successfully invaded France, pushing the Western Front back on the Germans. Hitler responded by ordering the launch of secretly developed vengeance bombs—V-1s— against Britain. The V-1 was a pilotless, jet-powered aircraft filled with high explosive. In truth, the Allies had known about the V-1 since 1943, when Polish resistance had smuggled out parts for analysis. The knowledge didn't help, as more than 9,500 V-1s were fired at Britain over four months, causing more than 22,800 civilian casualties.

The Abwehr called on their British agents to confirm that V-1s were hitting London. MI5 instructed double agents "Garbo," "Brutus," and "Tate" to give false information, ensuring many V-1s fell short, saving thousands of lives.

Advanced aircraft like this jet bomber were recovered from Nazi Germany during Operation Lusty.

SECRET ROUNDUPS

The V-1 was followed by the V-2 rocket—the first ever long-range military ballistic missile. When Germany was threatened with invasion in 1943, Hitler had ordered all scientists and intellectuals back from the frontline to help develop advanced weapons that might stave off defeat. After the surrender on May 8, 1945, the OSS ran Operation Paperclip to secretly recruit as many German "brains" as possible, to help in the ongoing fight with the Japanese.

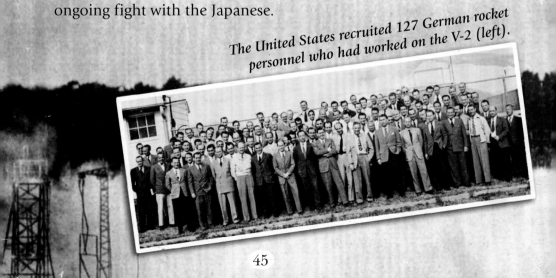

The United States recruited 127 German rocket personnel who had worked on the V-2 (left).

GLOSSARY

Allies The joint military forces fighting against Germany and Japan during World War II

assassin Someone who carries out a murder, often of a prominent person, by surprise attack

atomic bomb A devastating explosive device, deriving its energy from nuclear reactions; used by the US against Japan in August 1945

ballistic missile A guided missile that makes a high arc, then freefalls down

casualties Those in hostile engagements that die, are captured, or go missing

civilian A citizen who is not fighting in the army

clandestine Kept or done in secret; concealing something

convoy A group of ships traveling together to increase their safety

cyanide A form of poison, often used to commit suicide

decipher To figure out the meaning of something

detonate To explode something

Enigma The code used by Germany and its allies to send important messages during the war

exfiltrate To escape in secret from an area controlled by an enemy

exile To be sent away from one's native country

fuselage The main body of an aircraft, holding cargo or crew and passengers

A Japanese light carrier is hit during the Battle of the Coral Sea—the first time decyphered Japanese naval code gave the US an advantage in the Pacific.

guerrilla Undercover, irregular forces, often attacking an enemy by surprise

infiltrate To gradually enter or become established in a group or organization for the purpose of gaining military intelligence

liberation To be released from occupation by a foreign power

locomotive The engine that provides a train's power

magazine The storage space for ammunition in a firearm

morse code Either of two codes using dots and dashes or short and long signals

partisan A person or a group of people who harass an enemy

Pearl Harbor The location of Japan's surprise attack on the US in December 1941

reprisal An act of retaliation against an enemy, with the intention of inflicting more injuries than those received

resistance A movement fighting against occupying forces

rotors The rotating wheels used in machines that deciphered the Enigma code

sabotage A deliberate action aimed at weakening an enemy

sentry A soldier acting as a guard

SOE The abbreviation of Special Operations Executive

starboard The right-hand side of the plane

suicide To take one's own life

tender A car attached to a steam locomotive for carrying a supply of fuel and water

OSS agents prepare to board a B-24 as part of Operation Jedburgh in 1944. The 300 Jedburghs were supplied by the US, Britain, and Free France.

INDEX

35